Th Collection

Applied Theatre edition with exercises

Jennifer S. Hartley

© 2005, 2006, 2011, 2012, 2013 Jennifer S. Hartley

ISBN: 9798664090185

All rights reserved. No part of this publication may be reproduced, stored in retrieval system, copied in any form or by any means, electronic, mechanical, photocopying, recording or otherwise transmitted without written permission from the publisher. You must not circulate this book in any format.

Performance rights are the property of the author Jennifer S. Hartley. A performing fee is payable per performance on all plays.

For permissions contact: www.wearetvo.com or theatreversusoppression@gmail.com for rates and permissions.

Cover design by Mili Ortiz of Multi Story Media Ltd. (www.multistorymedia.co.uk)

Contents

Introduction	Page 1
The Art of Silence	Page 5
Workshop discussions & exercises	Page 49
The Sin Eater	Page 61
Workshop discussions & exercises	Page 95
'til Death do us Part	Page 107
Workshop discussions & exercises	Page 153
Sold	Page 163
Workshop discussions & exercises	Page 206
Inside Out	Page 217
Workshop discussions & exercises	Page 267
Conclusion	Page 277

Introduction

Theatre of the Oppressed and Applied Theatre plays are still theatre and as such should be engaging and entertaining for both participant and spectator. They should also be challenging, forcing us out of our comfort zone, necessitating that we think about what is occurring and how it could apply in our own lives. It is the role of the facilitator/writer to ensure that the theatricality of the plays is never lost. Only in this way will people believe in what they see and be willing to partake in the Applied Theatre journey. Our plays are written following techniques of Theatre of the Oppressed and Applied Theatre. By this I do not mean Forum. The moment a piece of Forum Theatre is written as a complete play, it is no longer Forum Theatre as in forum it is the audience who experiment with the outcome. It is a live and constantly evolving event. When I talk about the plays being Theatre of the Oppressed, I am referring to the fact that they were created, developed, directed and acted using Theatre of the Oppressed and Applied techniques.

The plays are always based on true stories. The design of the work and the steps taken to build these plays, ensure that the environment for participants is a safe one. It is this safe environment that allows participants to explore sensitive issues and ensure that relationships always feel real for them. Theatre allows safety and protection from the immediacy of the issue, while being real enough for the investigation into the issue to take place in a believable way. While some names and facts may be changed for the protection of those involved, the words are largely those of the participants and they all have a say in how the play is developed.

All of these plays follow certain rules and guidelines not only in how they are created but also in the format and presentation they take. There must always be a purpose behind creating the play – a reason for it existing and a reason why the audience is being exposed to these stories.

The plays tend to be minimalistic in terms of set, props, lights and cast size. From my personal experience, there are two reasons for this. Firstly, the script must be strong and powerful enough to both capture attention and to suggest all that is missing. Suggestion and the imagination are far more powerful than anything we can ever physically show on stage and it allows the audience their own personal journey. Each audience member will have a unique experience. Secondly the plays must be easily performed in a variety of locations, rarely theatres, where there will be no access to elements such as stage and lights. I have performed these theatre plays in locations as diverse as prison, secure mental health units, fields, malls, schools and universities, garages, shops, buses and streets. Often the space used is so small that the audience is tightly packed around making exit problematic. The sense of feeling trapped is often key to the issue being dealt with, the audience empathising with the story through their own discomfort.

The plays tend to be one act. An interval interrupts the process and can become a safety blanket for the audience, or a chance to escape from something that has taken them out of their comfort zone. The actors are often instructed to regularly address the audience directly, ensuring they make eye contact with individuals. The goal is to make the audience complicit in the events of the play both by their reactions, or lack of them. It is not intended to be a comfortable viewing experience for the spectators. At times audience members utter responses to the questions asked them by the actors, some wanting to justify their own reactions. The actors are strictly instructed to ignore this and not engage with the audience reactions during the plays.

A final point is that the plays are always accompanied by a talkback session with the audience, enabling them the opportunity to question, share, reflect, or simply to exhale. A talkback is a crucial processing and reflection phase for the audience, actors and also for the facilitators involved in the project. New questions are often raised and in answering them, we increase our own understanding of what has often been an intuitive process. The audience's reaction and commentary often give us a deeper insight into the issue being presented. This in turn informs our work as we proceed, enriching it in the process. While the scripts are created from the stories released through the projects, I usually take on the role of writer and director. In reality the writing is a shared process and stories, or extracts from them, are never used without the consent of those involved.

The plays afford us the opportunity to look at how we see things based on our own reactions, knowledge and emotions; how at times we see things as we desire them to be, rather than as they actually are, because it reinforces our own sense of righteousness or security. This extends to how we hear things; the way we selectively retain things heard or change the tone with which they were originally said to alter intent and meaning; the way we hear things that were never actually said. The plays are written with the intention of presenting the facts of the story, rather than apportioning blame to any individual. In most of our work we are aiming to show both sides of an issue in an attempt to understand human behaviour and actions. The audience are often left feeling complicit, as they realise that no situation is as black and white as it may seem: the behaviour can be condemned but the reasons behind the behaviour begs to be understood if a way forward is to be found.

In 2012 I released the book *Applied Theatre in Action: a journey*. This provides detailed examples of the projects created in which some of these plays were used and the exercises that accompanied them. It is recommended that this collection of plays be read in conjunction with that book to get an overall picture of this kind of work and approach to theatre.

The Art of Silence

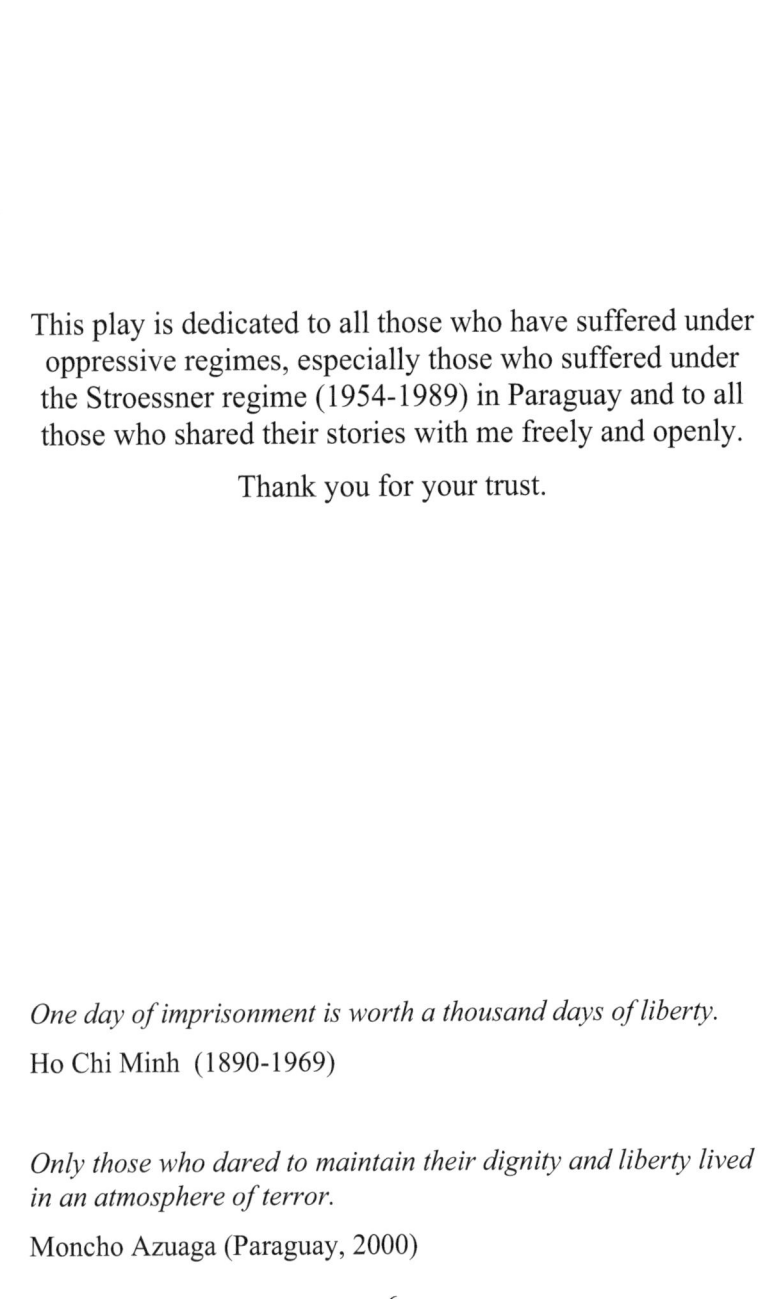

This play is dedicated to all those who have suffered under oppressive regimes, especially those who suffered under the Stroessner regime (1954-1989) in Paraguay and to all those who shared their stories with me freely and openly.

Thank you for your trust.

One day of imprisonment is worth a thousand days of liberty.

Ho Chi Minh (1890-1969)

Only those who dared to maintain their dignity and liberty lived in an atmosphere of terror.

Moncho Azuaga (Paraguay, 2000)

Introduction

In 1999 I began a series of interviews for my thesis with various theatre practitioners in Paraguay. Many were suspicious of both my work and intentions and, as a result unwilling to talk. But others did speak with me and provided an invaluable insight into their life in theatre in Paraguay. Many of these interviews stayed with me after I finished my thesis and I realised I had used only a fraction of the material gathered. Moreover, I felt that it had been a privilege to be given such information and therefore only right that I seek a way to make further use of it. I wanted to find a more direct and personal way to share the thoughts, the personalities, the lives, that I had been honoured to have glimpsed.

Time and again my thoughts came back to one man, Emilio Barreto. He had made such an impression on not only me personally, but also on my work as a theatre practitioner. Since carrying out the initial interviews, I had worked with many others who had been political prisoners in other countries and suffered severe oppression and torture Yet it was Emilio's story that made the biggest impact - what he had gone through, his rage, his sense of injustice. It seemed obvious to me that the next piece of writing I would do would be about Emilio. And so I wrote a play based Emilio's experiences in the *calabozo*[1].

While Emilio gave his permission to write the play, I doubt either of us ever considered the roller coaster of emotions we would go through in realising it. Writing the play was at times complex because I wanted something that would speak to all those oppressed by a political system, yet at the same time remain true to Emilio's memories and

---

[1] A 'calaboza' – a kind of prison cell often compared to a dungeon due to its small size, poor conditions and lack of windows and light.

experiences. To then go on to direct the play with Emilio playing himself in it was one of the most incredible and difficult experiences that I've had as a playwright and director. It is one I feel privileged to have taken part in, and one I am sure has marked my work ever since.

The play has a number of purposes: to act as a memory of atrocities that occurred in recent memory, atrocities for which only a handful of scapegoats were punished. To serve as a mark of respect to all those who stand up against oppression in any way they can. It is also a gift to Emilio and his family to thank them for sharing with me, welcoming me, teaching me and reminding me always to believe in, and stand up for, my principles.

Old Emilio: I was not brave.

Young Emilio: I am not a coward

Old Emilio: They are not the same thing.

These lines from the play for me represent the horror that those such as Emilio lived through and their strength of character to do more than survive. Silence is indeed an art but the time to be silent has long since passed in Paraguay. May the silent screams cease and the dialogue begin.

Thank you to all those who have helped me on my personal journey, reminding me that there is always more to learn, that there is always time to grow.

Prologue

Bent over a clean sheet of paper, preparing to write the preface of this theatre piece written by the theatre practitioner Jennifer Hartley, suddenly I felt, in my pen and on my shoulders, the enormous metaphysical weight of cowardice, of the art of silence in order to survive, the public shame, the ethical responsibility of all playwrights. Shame for having kept silent, shame for still being silent when facing the censure that that era of indignity and humiliation signified, of torture as the method and evil art of oppression and of imposed silence. Shame for all those who today, arrogant and unpunished declare aloud their totalitarian excesses and yearn for the dictatorial past, and in their nostalgia claim that we were all happy and just did not know it. Blind to the pain of the victims, cynically deaf to the clamour and the screams of those who were cruelly sacrificed in the dark cells –'the tombs of the living' - of the Investigations Department, of the Office of Technical Affairs, of all the Police Departments, of those who claimed to be defenders of peace and progress.

A lot of us kept silent and plotted the art of silence as the price to be paid for peace and survival, or there were those who complied with the police in order to obtain the crumbs that fell from the powerful table of terror and corruption. Emilio Barreto, student, mime-artist, actor, popular singer, teacher, a true Paraguayan who loves his country, insightful, wise, good hearted, an honest worker, suffered for thirteen years under the ominous and violent claws of tyranny that attempted to yield his spirit of solidarity and rebellious words. Faced with this reality, the majority of the population closed their eyes and ears to what was happening, claiming that the violations of human rights denounced were simply a defamatory campaign against the Superior Government. Politicians' banter - lies and fiction.

Paraguay was an oasis of peace, a heavenly country – well that is if you were an artist at hiding words, facts, concealing truths, building mute palaces, blind scenery, false laughter, plastic summertime. Pretending that the nocturnal assaults and the kidnappings of the honest and brave citizens perpetrated by the police and military did not exist. It was prohibited to talk about the terrible murders of political prisoners, the violent repression and death of the peasants, the persecution and exile of workers, educators and students. The rapes, cattle stealing, thefts, the excesses that were all committed by the complying politicians, were considered acts of defence of the status quo and anyone who spoke out against those acts was punished as an enemy of the state.

The art of silence was cultivated by playwrights, writers, politicians, businessmen, journalists, students, housewives, farmers, neighbours, friends, partners and lovers. Only in some catacombs, where the dignity of citizenship took refuge, was the ominous art of silence and submission despised. Only those who dared to maintain their dignity and liberty lived in an atmosphere of terror.

But Emilio never stayed quiet.

He paid with thirteen years of prison for such defiance.

And still that voice is kept in prison.

Emilio Barreto is still in prison - a prison that is made from the Paraguayan mentality that refuses to recognize the truth about the Stroessner dictatorship and still continues to give impunity to the executioners. Before the fall of the dictatorship, on the morning of 3rd January 1989, the claims of Emilio fell on deaf ears. The fear, the cynical deafness if not the brutal and selfish inference contradicted the reality pointed out by Emilio. And we justified such silence. And now in times of public liberties, with the well-publicized democracy that voice should multiply itself, become enormous before the evidence of an ominous reality that really did exist beneath the putrid hiding-cloak of governmental appearances.

However, it is not so yet. Despite the discovery and public exhibition of the Terror Archives, and the many condemnations, interviews, books, dossiers, that uncovered the true state and proved that Emilio Barreto was speaking the truth and that his fight in defence of the dignity of each citizen was legitimate, most of our society continued and continues feeding the shameful lie of the art of silence. This hypocritical society still refuses to look itself in the mirror and uncover its previous reality, it still fades, pretends, deforms, its modern reality. Before, it did not want to believe in the barbaric nature of its governors, in the ruling of torture, in the mutilated life imposed by those who exerted their despotic and volatile power. And today, they still refuse to believe.

What is worse is that some sectors of society, endorsed by the silence of others, recall the efficiency of the repression, the torture and exile as a positive method of social control. Social schizophrenia, the fragmentation of the public conscience and the loss of the collective memory, apart from the postmodern interests that emerge in the process of democratic transition, constitute walls that grow and hinder the discovery of the true history of our people. Crimes and political abuse are diminished, the violence of the despot is justified, the responsibility of judge and executioner is forgotten. The fate of the victim is a mere irony. To protest, to think different, to rebel is all Satanized. In other words, the unbelieving social spirit is more willing to risk repeating the history than admit the truth. Nostalgically, we wish to return to the labyrinth and summon the same, identical monsters. Zealously, we preserve the memory dictatorships, maybe because we are afraid of abandoning the irresponsible art of silence. When will we ever listen to the cries of our civilian heroes, of our popular artists imprisoned?

Today, a cultural investigator, Jennifer Hartley, an intelligent, beautiful, Scottish woman of the stage, a writer, director and practitioner, offers us in The Art of Silence that decomposed social face, very rarely assumed by national playwrights. It an excellent piece of theatre, an excellent piece of dramatic structure, based on Emilio Barreto's memories of his imprisonment.

Young Emilio and Older Emilio stand up to try to understand the irrational, the brutal, the absurd rule of General Stroessner and his henchmen's repressive system. Theatrical fiction to represent a reality that was denied its proper time by being considered fiction; a reality today that was understood as fiction yesterday. A cruel paradox. The political prisoner, confined in a real prison; the same prisoner, an actor in his own life, Emilio Barreto, incarnating himself. Confined within his own history. The fiction–reality interpolates the reality–fiction.

Jennifer provokes and challenges us. The Art of Silence, evokes, recreates and constructs in the spectators, the readers, the citizens, the accomplices, the executioners, today as well as yesterday, in the audience, in us, the Paraguayan society, the assumption of a civil responsibility for the ominous past and our confused future. From the stage, with dramatic rigor and stoical intention, distanced from social resentment, and a pamphletarian approach, the play defies indifference, fear and silence - because we are still cynical, cowardly, fearful or with evident selfishness, cultivating such wants, sheltering in muteness, in forgetfulness. The Art of Silence is not only a dramatic text, it is a live piece of our recent history, a still open wound in Paraguayan society.

Without doubt, Jennifer, with her original and authorized perspective, enriches local playwriting with The Art of Silence and incites us to a profound revision of our theatrical practices signalling the rich veins of the very near reality where fiction hides its theatrical shapes predisposed to dignify life. Our thanks to Jennifer, for this ethical provocation from the theatrical mixture of reality and fiction, our gratitude for reminding us of the necessity of recognizing our misery in public and the great civil courage of people of the stature of Emilio Barreto, a Paraguayan popular artist, whose fight surpasses the limits of the stage and becomes thought, pain and hope of the Paraguay we dream of.

Moncho Azuaga (April 2005)

Characters & Background

Older Emilio   (aged in his mid to late 20s)
Young Emilio   (aged late 60s early 70s)

While this play is based on the experiences of Emilio Barreto's imprisonment, there has been considerable adaptation to create this performance, because the innocent continue to suffer while the guilty walk free. The truth of events for all those who suffered under the Stroessner regime – under any oppressive regime - exists in the words of the play. Emilio's truth remains his own.

The play is set within the confines of a *calabozo,* a prison cell approximately four by two and a half metres, with no window, from which those like Emilio were allowed out once a week and which he shared with up to 18 others at times. The *calabozo* is marked only by changes in light to define size, restriction and mental confinement exhibited through the inner struggle of the younger Emilio to cope with his situation and the older to deal with his memories and comfort himself. Older Emilio moves around more freely with a more flexible light but in a distinct location from his younger self. Throughout, the younger Emilio is unaware of the presence of his older self who continually tries to communicate with and comfort him. They seem to acknowledge one another at certain moments but then they pass.

The jokes, stories and escape ideas are referred to but not detailed. The idea is that the actors create these in rehearsal and keep them alive and fresh by changing them regularly without telling one another. These moments of humour are essential in such a dark play for both the audience and the actors.

Lights up.

Both characters are sitting hugging their knees, rocking back and forth, facing the audience in different directions, each in their own 'cell'.

O. Emilio One, two, three, four, five ...

(Both count at other times throughout the play, regardless of any other words being spoken. Numbers increase at all times but not systematically one after another)

Y. Emilio You begin by counting the hours, then the days, then it becomes, weeks, months and finally years, until the desperation that lingers inside disappears replaced by a monotonous routine of counting. Like counting sheep at night, trying to fall asleep. You become so bored of waiting for sleep to come ... yet you continue counting because you're powerless to do anything else.

O. Emilio Nine, ten, eleven, twelve... *(Gets up frustrated pacing the confines of the cell and then sinks to the floor with his head in his hands).* I've become so accustomed to looking back, trying to disentangle it all, to find a real beginning *(directed at audience, with irony)* ... I have to be careful or I may forget how to look forward.

Y. Emilio Charged ... political prisoner ... but there's no charge ... so I'm not charged ... so I'm not a prisoner ... so this is not a prison ... *(laughs sarcastically)*

O. Emilio	*(mimicking the guards)* You're a fucking communist *(spits in Y.Emilio's face)* that's what you are!
Y. Emilio	*(anger sinking into disbelief, even despair)* And if I'm not a prisoner ... what am I? Where am I? Have they made me disappear? Have I ceased to exist? Can I disappear from my own life as if I never even existed? Can they do that?
O. Emilio	Of course they can! And you know it could all happen again. You think not, but I know. *(Sits back down and continues counting and will do so throughout the play although not marked hereafter)*
Both	22nd of June 1965. 22nd June 1965.
Y. Emilio	That's when they took me.
O. Emilio	*(irritated)* Kidnapped you! They didn't take you, you fool, both of you!
Y. Emilio	We'd only been married four months, no time to start a family ... and now I fear for the children I might never have. I mourn the unborn children I have lost.
O. Emilio	*(distracted and distant)* When you remember, it's distant, far away from you. *(laughing)* Someone else's story, *(signifying young Emilio with his head)* like that poor bastard's over there! *(Laughs)*
Both	*(muttering to themselves)* Silent screams ... silent screams ... our silent screams ... our silence.
Y. Emilio	I used to believe in God, but that was a long time ago. Not now! Now I can't. *(Getting*

	angry) How can I believe in the God they taught us about as children, the one we knelt in church to pray to? *(Cynically)* That God abandoned me a long time ago.
O. Emilio	But I believe in other things, in nature, in the sky and the earth, the God inside of us *(pause)* in my indigenous ancestors ...
Both	I believe in many things...
Y. Emilio	*(defiantly)* But not in Him!
O. Emilio	*(smiling tenderly at his younger self)* Defiance betrays you my friend. But that is *our* secret. The hurt is greater, the need to understand greater because we *do* believe.
Y. Emilio	*(laughing sarcastically)* Don't they say the closest thing to an atheist is a true believer? *(Pauses self-consciously in the middle of his own laughter, silence, shifts around, becoming agitated)* Dates. Names. Stories. I repeat them in my head. Over and over. Mustn't forget.
O. Emilio	*(turning away from his younger self and covering his ears)* Don't want to remember.
Y. Emilio	Over and over. Mustn't forget.
O. Emilio	Don't want to remember. *(Moves closer to Y.Emilio and sits huddled, almost whispering)* Tell them about the *pileta*, the famous *pileta*. *(laughs softly)*
Y. Emilio	*(animated begins to talk and slowly older Emilio joins in with action and gradually shares the dialogue)* The smell alone makes you sick. A bath filled with water, urine, menstrual blood, excrement, vomit ... your

	own, those who went before you ... they strip you naked to shame you, or leave you clothed so the putrid smell clings to your clothes. Feet strapped. Arms tied behind back. One straddles our knees. Another stands on our feet.
O. Emilio	*(getting excited in his acting out, an excitement that covers the pain and separates the memory from its personal link for the moment)* No squirming. No escape.
Y. Emilio	And then they pull you back and under! *(Pause)*
O. Emilio	Back and under! *(Pause)*
Y. Emilio	How long do you think you could hold your breath? *(Both take a deep breath and hold)* We practice, we calculate and we get better each time. *(Older Emilio continues to act this out)* But they realize and ...
O. Emilio	Bahm!
Y. Emilio	Punched in the groin. Mouth opens to scream. Pain. Swallowing. Gulping. Spitting. Vomiting. In your mouth. In your eyes. Up your nose. No air. Gasping. Gasping for breath and ...
O. Emilio	Bahm!
Y. Emilio	Punched in the stomach. Air running out. Gasping. Gasping. The smell. Swallowing. Choking. Choking and ...
O. Emilio	Bahm!
Y. Emilio	Another punch. Pain excruciating. Relinquish. Open mouth. Let go. Swallow.

	No more fight. No more struggle. Let death come. Peace. *(Repeats to older Emilio as a question)* Peace? No! *That's* when they pull you out and throw you on the floor.
Both	*(moving around agitated, muttering)* Silent screams ... silent screams ... our silent screams ... our silence.
O. Emilio	*(said with a sense of accomplishment)* Ready to give up. That's the way they like it. Broken.
Y. Emilio	Dead means failure. Dead means they have no more fun! *(Silence, they both stare at one another for some time)*
O. Emilio	*(mechanically spoken, no feeling)* They don't want you to die. They want you to suffer.
Y. Emilio	... that's what a torturer does ...
O. Emilio	... but you learn through the pain, through the beatings ...
Y. Emilio	... you learn about the world of these fascist animals.
O. Emilio	... Animals? No! Demons!
Y. Emilio	*(frustrated and desperate)* ... They are not human – they have no humanity. Demons, fascist demons!
O. Emilio	... you learn of their impotence through yours.
Y. Emilio	Suffer. Scream. Cry. Beg ... Beg for forgiveness.

Both	*(muttering agitation building)* Silent screams ... silent screams ... our silent screams ... our silence. *(long pause)*
Both	Beg for forgiveness.
O. Emilio	Forgiveness? For what?
Y. Emilio	For the crimes you never committed?
O. Emilio	For a lack of guilt ...
Both	Beg for forgiveness.
Y. Emilio	To end what is just beginning.
O. Emilio	To start anew.
Both	Beg for forgiveness.
Y. Emilio	From the animals who degrade us.
O. Emilio	From a God who doesn't exist.
Y. Emilio	The fear!
O. Emilio	The pain!
Both	*(quietly)* The shame.
Y. Emilio	When they torture you, finally you have a chance to confront them ... at least to kick them, spit on them, scratch them, scream at them.
O. Emilio	Such impotence. The psychologists, the psychiatrists – they can't understand what is happening in that moment.
Y. Emilio	They analyse
Both	As they agonize
O. Emilio	And secretly criticize
Y. Emilio	Trying to communalize

O. Emilio	A commitment to compromise
Y. Emilio	And systematically de-emphasize
O. Emilio	Over *this* ...
Both	*(spoken very deliberately and emphatically)* ... our petrified paradise.
Y. Emilio	Our culture - absolute silence
Both	Unmoveable ... petrified
Y. Emilio	We live in a petrified paradise.
O. Emilio	Our horrors de-emphasised by white coats and politicians.
Y. Emilio	It escapes their logic, their rationality.
O. Emilio	It escapes all logic…
Y. Emilio	…all rationality
O. Emilio	I tell them what I have seen and they don't want to listen, they don't want to see. *(pause)* It is always easier to forget the past,
Y. Emilio	... easier to rewrite a past that they can live with, without the guilt. History is a commodity; it changes like fashion and the truth is never known.
O. Emilio	But who will rewrite my past? It is etched in my mind.
Y. Emilio	... a recording that plays over and over
Both	without respite!
Y. Emilio	But who will listen to my truth?
O. Emilio	They say, 'how that Emilio talks, on and on, he never stops' ... they call me a mad man, they mock my words, they mock me,

	lessening my truth and every day, more and more, I speak in silence. No one listens, and those who do …
Both	… no one hears!
Y. Emilio	But I must speak for the others, the ones who can't … their stories need to be told …
O. Emilio	I must speak to escape the silence, the prison in my head. *(pause)* And I a prisoner.
Y. Emilio	And I in prison.
Both	*(deflated)* Silent screams … silent screams … our silent screams … our silence.
O. Emilio	*(in disbelief)* They called me a liar.
Y. Emilio	*(sarcastically)* An exaggerated tale.
O. Emilio	*(in anger and disbelief)* What do they know? *(pause)*
Y. Emilio	*(as if suddenly remembering)* You always know when they're going to torture you. They tell you 'Emilio today you are not going to eat, no breakfast, no lunch, no dinner!' and that's your clue that they're going to torture you … *(sarcastically)* as if you could even call what they gave us food! And do you know why?
O. Emilio	… because they don't like it when you shit yourself and that's what happens when your stomach's full.
Y. Emilio	*(laughing)* You shit because your stomach's full.
O. Emilio	You hear them say 'Tonight I have to work', that's what they call torture – work!

Y. Emilio *(mimicking the torturers)* 'I don't want to work with shit. Tell the boss not to feed the ones to be tortured or else they can come and do it themselves. I don't know why we can't just kill them!'

O. Emilio We ask the same – we wanted no more, we asked for no less. *(gently as a parent might speak of a child, acting out the process with his younger self)* And after our comrades would come back to the cell, we cleaned them, we washed them ... when they allowed us. We had nothing but our urine and our torn rags. But we tried.

Y. Emilio *(bitterly)* You feel so impotent because if you want to save your life, confronted with four, five, six torturers you have to accept it, but you can't and finally you explode and you try to just ... just kick them or spit on them or scratch them, you need to try to make it mean something. Make your life mean something...anything.

Both You have to try to fight back

Y. Emilio Because the torturers, they talk then and say, 'how terrible is 'so and so'! How strong he is! Did you see how he reacted? He's a hard one! I don't know that we can break that one!'

O. Emilio ... and you gain a sense of self and dignity

Y. Emilio ... as their words permeate the bruises, the cuts, the burns, the rotting festering sores, our gangrenous bodies

O. Emilio ... and the broken bones, don't forget the broken bones. *(Silence. whispering)* Silent

	screams ... silent screams ... our silent screams ... our silence. *(Directed at young Emilio)* What are you saying? We've got no time for silence! No time! There's so much to tell. *(shouting at Y.Emilio who cannot hear him)* Tell them! *(Angrily)* Remember for *them* ... *(despondently)* remember for me ... for us ... please you must remember.
Y. Emilio	Lying there gasping for breath and the doctor comes. *(Without emotion – older Emilio acting the part)* Check - pulse... heart ... pressure. No more today for this one. Ten, fifteen minutes more here, his heart can take it.
O. Emilio	*(said with emphasis)* How we hated them.
Y. Emilio	And all the time another in the *pileta* – no time to waste ...
O. Emilio	*(Mocking the guards once again)* ... far too many of 'you' fucking communists to get through ... *(laughs bitterly)*
Y. Emilio	Process the communist bastards. Break them or kill them. That's the policy. We long for death, plead with them to kill us. End it all. We would welcome death with open arms. If only they'd let us, if only ...
O. Emilio	And in those moments after the torture ...
Y. Emilio	*(wincing)* You relive it over and over again
O. Emilio	Reliving each bout of torture
Both	While waiting for the next.
Y. Emilio	*(wincing)* As you listen to the others
O. Emilio	Your comrades

Y. Emilio   Screaming in pain

O. Emilio   *(wincing)* As they are tortured. And you cover your ears and wish...

Y. Emilio   ... you wish it was you instead...

O. Emilio   *(quietly)* I wasn't brave.

Y. Emilio   *(in rage)* I am angry! Furious!

O. Emilio   *(quietly)* I was not brave.

(Pacing agitated, both stop, look at each other placing their hands over their ears and pacing more, older Emilio sinks to the floor)

Y. Emilio   *(tension building)* Worse ... worse ... listen to the others, their screams. Listen to their indignity, their pain. *(Voice rising, more agitated)* Worse ...worse ...listen to the silent screams ... *(older Emilio screams silently)*. And the beatings, the constant beatings of the silent ones. *(pause)*

O. Emilio   *(unwillingness to remember, inability to forget, speaks in a staccato manner)* The beatings ... you hear ... like dry blows ... clubs ... made of cow hide ... the whip ... they call it the lizard's tail ... tied together with metal balls at the end to rip your skin ... the sound *(pauses flinching)* the sound ... it tears the wind *(makes the sound)*

Y. Emilio   ... rips it in pieces

O. Emilio   *(pause)* ... like our skin.

Y. Emilio   The sound is almost metallic and then, suddenly, it disappears in the air. *(Older Emilio makes the sound repeatedly and*

	faster each time and then suddenly stops. Long pause, both frozen.)
O. Emilio	*(continuing as normal)* It is more painful than being beaten by wood because it cuts you …
Y. Emilio	… slices you
O. Emilio	And leaves a deeper wound.
Y. Emilio	But worst of all are the beatings on the soles of your feet because they reverberate to your head as the bones break one by one … it's like
O. Emilio	… bells pealing!
Y. Emilio	Metal bells – solid iron.
O. Emilio	And *they* know it!
Y. Emilio	They always know!
O. Emilio	Some even named their whips …
Y. Emilio	… makes it all a little more personal
Both	an act among friends
O. Emilio	The chief of police had two whips, he called one 'The national constitution' and the other 'Human rights' *(laughs shaking his head, stops and turns to younger Emilio with a changed expression as he takes on the role of the chief of police).* So you are telling me that it's against your human rights to keep you here? You fucking communist, you think you have rights? You think you deserve to have rights? You are no one. Nobody! Who is looking for you? Who is

	fighting for you? Who will defend you and your human rights?
Y. Emilio	The national constitution says that you cannot . . .
O. Emilio	National Constitution! Friends, we're spoiled for choice *(he looks around supposedly at the other police laughing)* what's it to be your rights or the constitution? Or perhaps a taste of both. Let us start with your rights – Human rights *(shouts out the words as a command to have the whip brought to him)* – tell me what your human rights are, one by one so I can respond in full *(acts out whipping him)*. Is the discussion over or do you want to claim your rights under the national constitution?
Y. Emilio	And their laughter echoes
Both	The perversion of words
Y. Emilio	Here words can kill ... and they do
O. Emilio	They become weapons
Y. Emilio	Words to kill words
O. Emilio	*(continuing in the role of the chief of police)* You think you deserve to have rights? You are no one. Do you hear me? Nobody! Who is looking for you? Who is fighting for you? Tell me who will defend you and your human rights?
Y. Emilio	They are looking. *She* is looking, waiting ...
O. Emilio	And who was looking for her – who realised she was lost. I was in prison and she was free, but she was lost, lost in her own silence

	... (both reach out simultaneously as if to take 'her' in their arms. Long pause)
Both	*(with sadness, but asked in a way that expects no response)* What did they do to you? *(pause)* Forgive me.
O. Emilio	The more you try to avoid the suffering – the more you suffer. *(the following is spoken mechanically between the two)* I lost the sight in one eye.
Y. Emilio	I am deaf in one ear.
O. Emilio	They broke my kneecaps.
Y. Emilio	Metal bars, electric cattle prods, whippings, fire hoses, the *pileta* ...
O. Emilio	*(breaking in and screaming)* Stop! *(Both look at each other as if in shock and then with pain)* My shopping list ...
Y. Emilio	My shopping list ... is full. The shopping list of an unrealized tragedy.
O. Emilio	Unfinished my friend, unfinished. *(Then both laugh uneasily followed by a long pause, older Emilio turns away)*
Y. Emilio	*(all of the following is acted out)* They bury me alive, make me dig my own grave.
O. Emilio	The irony *(laughs shaking his head)*
Y. Emilio	Lazy bastards won't get their hands dirty. They take me out in the night, to the side of the river and give me a shovel and say ...
O. Emilio	Dig! Dig you bastard!
Y. Emilio	I don't realize I am digging my own grave, until they make me lie in it and the earth

	starts pouring over me as they shovel it back on top of me. *(Breathing becomes irregular, uncertainty and fear showing through).*
O. Emilio	*(voice rising, becoming more and more desperate to be heard)* The hand, reach out so they can find you.
Y. Emilio	Earth covering my chest, my legs, my face. In my mouth, starts to weigh me down. *(Breathing more sporadic and irregular)*
O. Emilio	The hand! They have to find you ... later. They have to know you are dead.
Y. Emilio	*(desperate, breathing badly, as if suffocating)* And if they bury me here no one will know and they will keep looking and looking, never knowing if I am dead.
O. Emilio	*(also desperate – reaching out towards his younger self as if to take his hand)* The hand! Reach out my friend.
Y. Emilio	And I reach out my hand as they cover my body. Someone will find my body. Someone will tell my wife. She can stop looking. *(pause)* She can stop hoping.
O. Emilio	*(walking away, shaking his head but speaking to himself)* Don't be one of the disappeared ones. The dead that can never rest.
Both	The unknown dead.
O. Emilio	Lost forever.
Y. Emilio	And then they stop. I hear their laughter. They pull me up and laugh at my tears. But I don't cry for fear of death, or fear of them

	– cowards that they are - I cry for fear of being a disappeared one. And on they laugh, poking me with the butts of their rifles, calling me a coward ... *they* called *me* a coward.
O. Emilio	*(quietly)* I wasn't brave.
Y. Emilio	*(in rage)* I am no coward!
O. Emilio	*(quietly)* They are *not* the same thing. That much I have learned. *(Long pause)*
Y. Emilio	*(in rage)* I am no coward! *(Pause, a mixture of anger, frustration and sadness)* I want a strength that denies pity, I don't want them looking at me with pity. I don't want *her* looking at me with pity.
O. Emilio	It will come, it will come. *(Pause)* At a price that not all can pay.
Y. Emilio	And she?
O. Emilio	She will carry you through her silence.
Both	The art of silence.
Y. Emilio	And she ...
O. Emilio	... she will never tell her story. It will dissolve in yours.
Y. Emilio	Her silence
O. Emilio	Our silence
Both	*(whispering to one another)* Silent screams ... silent screams ... our silent screams ... our silence.
O. Emilio	And I a prisoner.
Y. Emilio	And I in prison.

Both	*(moving closer voices rising)* Silent screams ... silent screams ... our silent screams ... our silence.
Y. Emilio	*(sudden shift in tempo)* So who ... what would you be, turn yourself into to escape from here?
O. Emilio	The games we played.
Y. Emilio	Imagine anything ... but you have to show how you'd do it.
O. Emilio	When you're in prison you think about escape ... every minute of the day ...
Y. Emilio	... how ... when ... where ...
Both	A game you play with yourself. Planning every move.
O. Emilio	If not we'd just be animals in a cage.
Y. Emilio	Pacing.
O. Emilio	Waiting.
Both	Forgotten.
O. Emilio	*(acting out the roles of fellow prisoners in turn with their ideas)* I'd be an ant *(explains and acts out his escape)*. I'd be smoke *(explains and acts out his escape)*. Invisible ... *(laughter, the list continues)*.
Y. Emilio	*(defiantly)* I'd be some kind of superhero – no, better still a 'super'-duck and when they took me to the *pileta* I 'd swallow the lot ... every last drop and then ... *(acting it out)* then I'd spit it in the face of my torturer *(they laugh loudly and then suddenly stop, both self-aware. They look at each other for a*

	period of time and slowly move to face each other as if looking in a mirror. They each trace the lines on their own faces simultaneously)
Y. Emilio	Will I grow old here? Will I die?
Both	A thousand times over
O. Emilio	Will my body break?
Both	A thousand times over
Y. Emilio	Will my spirit stay strong?
Both	A thousand times over
Y. Emilio	As the years pass and the hope fades?
Both	A thousand times over
Y. Emilio	Will I live to tell this tale?
Both	A thousand times over
O. Emilio	Will they believe me?
Both	Will I? *(pause)*
Y. Emilio	Will the nightmares ever cease?
Both	A thousand times over
Y. Emilio	Will I ever be free?
O. Emilio	After they let me go, will I ever be free?
Both	*(with sadness)* Silent screams ... silent screams ... our silent screams ... our silence.
O. Emilio	And I a prisoner.
Y. Emilio	And I in prison. *(long pause)* I dream of freedom.
O. Emilio	I dream of prison.
Both	And I awake not knowing where I am.

O. Emilio	Am I free? Am I in prison?
Y. Emilio	Am I awake? Am I asleep?
Both	Am I still waiting? *(At opposite ends of the marked cell both thunder their fists on an imaginary wall)*
Y. Emilio	I want to awaken, but I don't know what I want to awaken to. And the nightmares ...
O. Emilio	They will never end my friend, never.
Both	Nightmares that never end. *(Young Emilio crouches in the corner of his cell in a foetal position as if asleep)*
Y. Emilio	I dream of dreaming.
O. Emilio	Wake up Emilio. Wake up my friend. *(Crawling towards the younger Emilio, whispering)* You are free. *(Pauses and turns to the audience)* And in my dreams, time and again I enter the *calabozo* one last time to see my companions. They come to embrace me. But when I awake ... I am free ... and my companions have gone.
Both	And I am alone now. *(Both sit rocking, hugging their knees. Pause.)*
Y. Emilio	*(building up to a fury)* Silent screams deafen me everywhere here
O. Emilio	The silent screams, the dry tears. The cries that are never heard.
Both	The unfinished stories. *(pause - intermittently speaking and acting out the gesture)* Silent screams ... silent screams ... our silent screams ... our silence.

O. Emilio	I have no motivation to remember.
Y. Emilio	I have no means to forget.
O. Emilio	They call me a survivor. *(Cynically)* What is survival? That I am not dead? Is this my achievement? How many of us survived if that is to be the only criteria?
Y. Emilio	Our techniques of survival.
O. Emilio	We had no choice.
Both	We were the forgotten ones
O. Emilio	Our games to survive
Y. Emilio	To pass the time
Both	The endless time
Y. Emilio	We play imaginary instruments and sing *(he acts this out and begins singing a typical song, laughing intermittently and getting louder each time)*
O. Emilio	We would sing and sing. How it annoyed them *(they laugh)* ... our festivals of pretence with our imaginary instruments ... instruments they could not break ...
Both	... as they broke our spirits
O. Emilio	... instruments they could not take away from us
Both	... as they took our freedom

(Older Emilio joins in the singing and instrument playing)

Both	Our need to make sound, to hear sound – sound that was not theirs.
Y. Emilio	... our 'keepers'

O. Emilio	... as they hid us away
Y. Emilio	... as they gagged us
O. Emilio	... as they castrated our tongues *(mimicking the anger of the guards)* Shut up! Shut up you bastards or we'll shoot you!
Y. Emilio	*(laughter)* Shoot us then – come on! We sing louder.
O. Emilio	They would bang on the iron door of the *calabozo* with their rifles. *(continuing to mimic the guards)* Stop it. Now!
Y. Emilio	*(laughing)* Come on in and shoot us – we're waiting!
O. Emilio	*(decisively)* We were hoping.
Both	Come join us!
O. Emilio	*(matter of fact)* They would never shoot us. *(pause)* They opened the door and threw in buckets of water ...
Y. Emilio	*(suddenly serious)* ... or sand in our faces ... *(acting out receiving the action)*
Both	*(tone has become more sombre)* ... they handcuffed us, they chained our feet.
Y. Emilio	*(lighter tone returning)* But still we sing, louder and louder *(they sing again)* What if they gag you?
O. Emilio	I will sing with my body ... with my eyes ... louder and louder ... time after time ... without tiring ... until my death ...
Y. Emilio	And then?
Both	And then? *(Both look at each other, then to the audience and begin to laugh)*

35

O. Emilio	*(caught up in the momentum, as if suddenly remembering with delight)* We would tell jokes
Y. Emilio	Jokes of every kind and colour *(Both, sitting back to back, in turn proceed to tell some typical jokes, laughing loudly at each one)*
Both	And we would tell jokes. *(pause)* Loudly.
O. Emilio	... so they would hear our laughter, so they would hear our spirit
Y. Emilio	... alive ... not broken ...
Both	... not yet . . .
O.Emilio	We wrote poetry ... even though we were not allowed pencil or paper.
Y.Emilio	We gave recitals, monologues, dialogues *(act out examples)* ... In that way we passed the days ...
Both	... the years. In that way …
O.Emilio	... we kept company with death.
Y. Emilio	There are different kinds of death. You die a thousand times over waiting for the day that they will come for you, because you know, you always know and you expect it and prepare for it …
O. Emilio	And still it takes you by surprise.
Y. Emilio	You die a thousand times over when they torture you until ... I reach a point when I feel no more ... the physical pain ... I don't feel it anymore …
O. Emilio	Are you already dead then? Is it possible we all died somewhere in the *calabozo*?

Y. Emilio	From a numbness of all feeling? You die a thousand times over as you count the days that never end. You die a thousand times over wondering about your family ...
O. Emilio	Are they searching? How will they know where to look? How will they find me? *(Pause)* Do they care? *(Pause)* Are they alive?
Y. Emilio	Are they dead like us, dead in their living? Everybody is afraid, nobody speaks and the innocent are too innocent.
O. Emilio	And the guilty are too guilty
Y. Emilio	I am too young
O. Emilio	I am too old
Y. Emilio	But we laugh as we cry, comrades in our great undignified dignity.
O. Emilio	*(speaking to younger Emilio as a fellow prisoner)* Tell me a story! *(back to the present)* We played at who could lie the most, to see whose lies were the most imaginative. It was practically like writing, creating stories, novels ... *(speaking to younger Emilio again)* Tell me a story!
Y. Emilio	... we have nothing else of which to speak.
O. Emilio	Otherwise we would lose our wings ...
Both	... our sense of imagination *(tempo change)*
O. Emilio	We would tell stories that would last for days
Y. Emilio	weeks
O. Emilio	We would wait each day for the next part

Y. Emilio	We have to find reasons
Both	To live
Y. Emilio	To wake
O. Emilio	To believe that there was more ...
Both	More than this.
O. Emilio	We have to find reasons.
Y.Emilio	To make sense
Both	Of this
O. Emilio	We have to find reasons
Both	To pass the time
Y. Emilio	to think
O. Emilio	not to think
Y. Emilio	of what lies ahead
O. Emilio	of the torture *(long pause, speaking to younger Emilio as a fellow prisoner)* Tell me a story! *(they begin to tell stories, each one tells a story)*
Both	Stories to pass the time
Y. Emilio	to think
O. Emilio	not to think
Y. Emilio	of what lies ahead
O. Emilio	of the torture
Y. Emilio	... and we have so many other worries, torture is just one more.
O. Emilio	... just one more in a world of silence ... we have so many other worries ...

Y. Emilio	*(throughout Young Emilio grows agitated, angry and distressed at times, while the older Emilio is reliving through action)* When to shit. Where to shit? Is there any toilet paper? Will there be food? Will they have spat in our food? Hidden their excrement in it? Will there be water to drink? Will it be clean? Will we have to drink our urine? How do we clean the wounds from our beatings? How do we stop the stench? Dirty t-shirts for bandages. Urine for antiseptic. How many in the cell today? Are my wounds turning gangrous? Is there space to lie down? How many will stay standing? Is anyone looking for me? Will I ever be free? The air thick with the putrid smell of rotting carcasses. The summer heat. How to stay clean? Will we have visitors? Will they be repulsed by us?
O. Emilio	... by the smell, by the sight of the unbreakable breaking. *(Pause)* They told us later how the smell repulsed them ...
Y. Emilio	They swallow mouthfuls of vomit as they sit with us, repulsed, talk with us ... minutes lasting hours in our silent conversations . . .
O. Emilio	... as they pretended we were still alive
Y. Emilio	As they try to hide their horror and look at us as if we are still whole.
O. Emilio	... unbroken
Y. Emilio	... but they never look us in the eye
O. Emilio	... as they tell us we will be free one day
Y. Emilio	... because they know

O. Emilio	... we will never be free again
Y. Emilio	... even when they let us go. *(Both stand diagonally apart from each other, a look of horror changing to one of resignation)*
Both	*(heads in hands)* Silent screams ... silent screams ... my silent screams ... my silence
Y. Emilio	*(rising defiantly, angrily addressing the audience)* I am not defined by prison, by my imprisonment, I am not the *calabozo* two and a half metres by four where I spend my years, with no window and the cracks in the door my only view of another world, splintered and narrow.
O. Emilio	*(calmer but with suppressed fury)* I am not the stifling smell of rotting bodies and decaying minds that share my space in moments of time; or the faeces and the urine neatly compacted in old used up tins of dried milk in the corner of a cell, festering in the heat, until they let us out to empty and clean them ... clean them in the toilets that we are not permitted the dignity of using.
Y. Emilio	*(building to a rage)* I am not a shadow that clings to the prison walls, I am not the sum of the indignities forced upon me by cowardice masking as obedience, cowardice that makes us bend ...
O. Emilio	*(makes a snapping noise and smiles, calmly)* or break! (Pause)
Y. Emilio	(calming down) I am not defined by their perversion of language, by this island without sea. *(Pause)* I will not be defined by those who sentence me

O. Emilio	without a crime
Y. Emilio	by those who condemn me
O. Emilio	without a trial
Y. Emilio	It is not
O. Emilio	It is not
Both	who I am!
Y. Emilio	Who am I?
O. Emilio	I may be silent
Y. Emilio	but thoughts resound in my head.
Both	The art of silence, a crescendo of silent voices.
Y. Emilio	I am imprisoned and my words are executed. I may be silent but I am thinking,
Both	a crescendo of silent voices.
Y. Emilio	Hidden thoughts
O. Emilio	Hidden within me.
Both	The art of silence.
Y. Emilio	The status of being labelled a political prisoner.
O. Emilio	*(sarcastically)* What does it mean to be a political prisoner?
Y. Emilio	A prisoner with politics, a prisoner with thoughts, political thoughts *(laughs)* what do they know of my thoughts? Do they ever ask? They have always told us what to think.
Both	*(shouting uncontrollably and simultaneously)* Fascists! *(pause, both staring out at the audience uncertain and*

	unsure of how to continue from their own outburst)
O. Emilio	*(walking around the space, with his hands signifying the cell)* Political prisoners are prepared for this ... they have ... they have a certain ...
Y. Emilio	... *we* have a certain level of instruction ... of training
Both	... of preparation
O. Emilio	*(sarcastically)* What does it mean to be a political prisoner?
Y. Emilio	*(in anger)* Imprisoned for my thoughts. What do they know of my thoughts? Did they ever ask? They tell us our thoughts ... tell us what to think.
O. Emilio	The lies of generations. *(Laughing sarcastically)* Moral decrepitude.
Y. Emilio	Truthful inaptitude.
O. Emilio	Mental ineptitude.
Y. Emilio	Shameful servitude.
O. Emilio	*(smiling)* Impoverished gratitude.
Y. Emilio	The magnitude of the nourishment of our dictators.
O. Emilio	Dependent upon our fear, nourishing it, ready for
Both	... the slaughter. *(Both slam their fists against the imagined prison wall)*
O. Emilio	And I a prisoner.
Y. Emilio	And I in prison.

Both	*(intermittently speaking and acting out the gesture)* Silent screams ... silent screams ... our silent screams ... our silence.

(There is a long pause and then the action shifts. Older Emilio takes on the persona of his fellow prisoners and as such the two Emilios now interact)

Y. Emilio	Imagine they gave us one wish, one desire what would you ask for
O. Emilio	... better food, medical attention, a bed, that we could wash ...
Both	One wish
Y. Emilio	For my freedom!
O. Emilio	Don't be a fool Emilio *(irritated)* why would you ask for your freedom, they're not going to give you *that*!
Y. Emilio	*(angrily)* No! No! I only want freedom, give me that and I can solve the problem of my food, I can get medical care, I ... *(older Emilio starts to shout him down, rejecting his ideas)*. If Christ Himself came here I would ask Him for my freedom, I would have to. That is the obligation of a prisoner – to fight for liberty. Do you think you can be content in the *calabozo* just because you can say ... bring me a doctor, bring me a damn ice cream, bring me an air-conditioner, build me a window ... oh please!
O. Emilio	*(slipping into the present again)* We were born for freedom.

Y. Emilio It's not freedom if my *calabozo* has an air conditioner or a window, or I have a bed, or a doctor to see me!

O. Emilio *(trying to calm him in the present and so unheard and unseen)* Calm yourself my friend. It was a game ... it is only a game my friend. It's all a game.

Y. Emilio *(lost in his own thoughts)* And when I walk around in the yard, in the free air, I have guards to stop me from escaping.

O. Emilio *(emphatically)* They are also imprisoned.

Y. Emilio And even out there, freedom is conditional; you are dependent upon what happens in this ...

Both ... immature society!

O. Emilio Our globalized prison!

Both Our prison is here *(tapping their heads)*

O. Emilio Prison is not the lack of air in the confining space

Y. Emilio It is not the lock and key and bolt on the door

O. Emilio It is not the lice that eat our scalp, the cockroaches that eat our skin, or the scabies that poison our wounds.

Y. Emilio It is not the singed embers of our beards. Burned with the rationed cigarette butts.

O. Emilio *(pausing pensively)* They did not let us wash or shave

Y. Emilio and the smell from our own bodies nauseates us beyond shame.

O. Emilio Prison is not the soiled food they shit in or the water they urinate in ... *(sudden change in tempo)* on the days we were fortunate enough to receive food and water.

Y. Emilio It is not the inability to define night from day in a darkened world, our deathly pale bodies

O. Emilio *(almost whispering)* Cadaverous Christs!

Y. Emilio *(begins almost as an aside but becomes almost vicious in the delivery of the lines)* The Christ painted in pictures, they always give Him some colour. *(cynically)* Is it possible that crucified, having lost so much blood ... bleeding ... bleeding from His cross ... that *He* had some colour in his face?

O. Emilio *(in cynical disbelief)* ... and *we* were ghosts, shadows against a wall?

Y. Emilio *(almost whispering)* Cadaverous Christs!

O. Emilio Prison is not the uneasy listening of the voices outside ... *(both move to edge of the cell listening intently, reaching out for someone who is not there. After a time before speech resumes)*

Y. Emilio ... and one imagines a child, a woman, a voice that is searching to prove we exist.

O. Emilio Prison is not out there.

Y. Emilio *(screaming out unable to control himself any longer, tears of frustration)* My prison is here *(slapping at his head violently)*

O. Emilio *(trying to distance himself from the other, unable to witness his pain)*... and I am never really free.

Y. Emilio *(suddenly calm, almost 'too' calm)* There are many things, so many things, that when I begin to tell seem no more than fantasy.

O. Emilio They called them fantasies, my stories of prison. They called me a liar. They wouldn't listen.

Y. Emilio I forgot how to speak. In prison I would not give them that privilege ... the privilege to hear me speak.

O. Emilio And then I didn't know where to begin. I would sit alone remembering, thinking about it all. But I have no motivation to remember. Not alone.

Y. Emilio Share the nightmare.

O. Emilio Pass it on a little. It's easier that way.

Y. Emilio What is wrong with us that we want to escape?

O. Emilio Where would we go?

Y. Emilio Could we ever be free?

O. Emilio *(decisively)* There's too much to tell. I have been silent too long.

Y. Emilio *(afraid)* But there's not enough time.

O. Emilio So many times they said they would set us free.

Y. Emilio So many times I dreamt of that day. And when it finally happened, it wasn't real *(clearly anguished)* ... it was just like a

	dream, one of the many dreams ... *(to the audience)* I waited to wake up.
O. Emilio	*(emphatically)* I'm still waiting. *(Pause)* 4,575, 4756, 4757, 4758, 4759.
Y. Emilio	15th of February 1978.
O. Emilio	15th of February 1978.
Y. Emilio	4,759, almost thirteen years.
O. Emilio	4,759, almost thirteen years.
Y. Emilio	I never felt a prisoner until the day they set me free.
O. Emilio	It was only then I began to see death everywhere I looked ... in the eyes of children.
Both	*(whispering loudly, anger building)* Silent screams ... silent screams ... our silent screams ... our silence.
Y. Emilio	*(sinking back into a corner of the calabozo, hugging his knees and rocking)* 15th of February 1978. 4,759, almost thirteen years. *(Older Emilio crosses over and takes up the same position, rocking side by side)*
Both	One, two, three, four, five ...
Y. Emilio	*(calmly)* You begin by counting the hours, then the days, then it becomes, weeks, months and finally years, until the desperation that lingers inside disappears replaced by a monotonous routine of counting. Like counting sheep at night, trying to fall asleep. You become so bored of waiting for sleep to come, yet you continue counting because you're powerless

Both ... powerless to do anything else. *(lights fade)*

The End

Continues for the Paraguayan version only:

(Pause. Both stop rocking and stand, looking at the audience)

Y.Emilio *(despondently)* ... we return to where we began.

O.Emilio And so the innocent continue to suffer and the guilty walk free: *(what follows passing from one to the other is a list of the names of every Paraguayan torturer who walked free – that is, in other words, all of them. They speak the names mechanically – adding comment of the 'nicknames' they were given for their torture 'speciality', no emotion.)*

Both *(intermittently speaking and acting out the gesture)* Silent screams ... silent screams ... our silent screams ... our silence. *(Lights fade)*

The End

Workshop Ideas

Below are discussion points and exercises that can help not only lead us to a better understanding of the play, but also of Applied Theatre and what it involves. In all Applied Theatre and Theatre of the Oppressed exercises, discussion is key. Always allow ample time for discussion after each exercise and explore what has happened.

Discussion questions

1. Discuss the stage elements of the play and what makes it Applied Theatre e.g. set, lights, props etc.
2. The concept of applied plays is not to take sides but simply to tell the story. How do our feelings about Emilio change throughout the play and why?
3. What evidence is there that Emilio's torture continues albeit in his own head? Why do you think this is?
4. What is the purpose of this play?
5. The set is designed to make the audience feel entrapped. How do you think this is achieved?
6. Discuss why you think Emilio wanted his story to be told.
7. In the introduction Emilio talks of a dream in which he saw himself smashing the writer's world in a symbolic way. Why do you think he felt this way?
8. Is Emilio a hero? Why/why not? What makes someone a hero?
9. What feelings is the writer trying to evoke in the audience and why?
10. What is the purpose of the alternative ending for Paraguay? How do you think people reacted to this ending and why?

11. The play suggests that the problem is 'silence' whether it be from the victim, perpetrator or onlooker. At many performances audiences discussed their own silence about things they had witnessed, or things that had happened to them. Applied theatre looks to make the audience consider how they have behaved in a similar way albeit in a different situation. Can you think of a time when you were silent? Would you change that now?
12. Moments of humour are key to many applied scripts in order to give the audience a moment of release. Look at the humorous moments in the play and what preceded them. Why was it so important to include humour at those precise moments?
13. Emilio reveals a sense of guilt about 'her'. Who is she and why do you think he feels this?
14. The minimal nature of Applied Theatre often means that the audience see things that are not there and do not happen in the play. Frequently audiences have insisted that they saw twenty people in the 'calabozo' even though there are only two actors; that they saw the elements of torture despite there being no props whatsoever in the play, that they saw the doctor come in to check the victims and so on. In talkbacks after the play audiences have been very insistent on these points. Discuss why this happens and how powerful a tool this can be in applied work.
15. When the audience laughs in applied theatre, they become complicit. What is meant by this?
16. It is normal for an Applied Theatre performance to have a discussion time with the audience after the play. Why do you think this is necessary?
17. It has been said that Applied Theatre plays with our emotion and our certainties. Discuss.
18. 'Older Emilio is jealous of his younger self and resents him.' Discuss this statement.

Applied Theatre Exercises

When doing these exercises it is important to remember that the different stages will often be carried out on different days and do not need to be done in succession. The exercises can be adapted and used for any of the plays.

Please note that in Applied Theatre time should *always* be allocated to discuss and process the exercises after they have been completed.

The 'calabozo'

Stage 1:   Mark out an area with tape or chalk measuring 4 metres by 2.5 metres. Play with an exploration of the space and how confining it can be through various exercises:

- Pace the space repeatedly to get a feel for its limiting size
- Add up to twenty people into the space and explore the limitations of movement and comfort
- Sit in the space with eyes closed for a lengthy period of time. Explore your senses in the space and how your thoughts begin to wander.

Discuss what you learned about the space; how it made you feel. Imagine spending thirteen years in this space, how do you think it would affect you?

Stage 2:   Sitting in the confines of the calabozo, the actors take it in turns to tell one another jokes. They can be any joke but they must keep the exercise going as long as possible.

Discuss the role of laughter in desperate situations. Discuss when you start running out of jokes, how does it make you feel? How does the laughter change the longer the exercise continues?

Stage 3: Within the confines of the calabozo the actors take turns to invent methods of escape. However as they tell one another their ideas they must act out the process.

Discuss why you think the prisoners liked this game, despite knowing that escape was impossible. What is the difference between escape and escapism?

Stage 4: Once again sitting within the confines of the calabozo the actors take it in turns to tell the greatest lie they can think of to one another. It is clearly a grandiose lie but the actor must tell it as convincingly as possible and act as though it is the complete truth. The others in the calabozo can question the truth of the lie by asking additional questions. The actor telling the lie must try to convince the others of the truth of his lie without being caught out by making a mistake or giving inaccurate information as proof.

Afterwards discuss the nature of truth and lies, especially in a situation like this. If we believe something, is it true?

Angel/Devil

In character, the actor speaks a monologue from the play. Seated behind him on either side are his angel and devil and they whisper his thoughts and intentions from their perspectives. They have no physical contact with the actor in the middle and must stay in their seats, so they must look for ways to make themselves heard. The actor tries to focus on his monologue and not be distracted by what he is hearing. Discussion with the whole group afterwards looks at what has happened and the changes which have occurred.

Do this for both young and old Emilio.

Variations

- the angel and devil are allowed to move around and have agreed upon contact with the actor in the middle
- rather than a monologue the actor in the middle simply explains his situation and then engages with the angel and devil as each tries to win him over to their way of thinking
- after some time the actor in the middle is removed and the angel and devil are left to argue out the situation between themselves
- the interaction between the angel and devil is changed – first one seated and the other standing but no physical contact; then reverse this; next both standing but no physical contact; finally allowing physical contact
- angel and devil are removed and the actor in character repeats his monologue or speaks about his current frame of mind as a result of what he has heard.

Images of a story

When doing these exercises it is important to remember that the different stages will often be carried out on different days and do not need to be done in succession.

Stage 1: One actor walks into the middle and freezes in a position from the play without speaking or explaining. The other actors interpret and join in with the image if they feel it is relevant. Note that while the play is only for two actors, multiple people may be involved in the images as the play often refers to others we do not see. When everyone who wishes to has joined the image it is held for a couple of minutes.

The physical pain from image work often felt in these exercises is intentional and can lead to a deeper understanding of character and intent. The physical pain also often mirrors the emotional pain of the character.

After a couple of minutes, still without speaking, the actors return to their places. Another then enters the middle with a new position and the process is repeated.

After repeating this several times, the group sit and discuss the work looking at how they interpreted the images and how it felt to hold the positions.

Stage 2: The process of stage 1 is repeated only this time each person entering the image, from the first, says one word. It is important at this stage that it is only one word. Throughout the time of creating and holding the image, each actor repeats the word over and over playing with tone and pitch. It is essential the actors remain frozen throughout.

After a period of playing with their word, the actors, still frozen, use their word to converse with one another. For example, one actor may use the word 'silence', another 'stop', another 'regrets' and another 'scared'. First, they will repeat these words over and over playing with tone and pitch, exploring the word in their own heads. Next they try to converse with the word so we might end up with: silence – scared – stop – silence – regrets – stop – silence – scared – regrets and so on. By playing with the volume and emotion of the words a conversation develops from the use of four simple words.

After repeating this several times, the group sit and discuss the work looking at if, and how, the meaning and depth of the images and situations changed with the use of the words. They should also discuss how it begins to affect their understanding of the characters and their stories.

Stage 3: The process of stage 1 is repeated only this time each person entering the image, from the first, says a sentence relevant to what is happening in the image. For example a sentence may be, 'I can't take it anymore', or 'I am not a coward'. The next person also says a sentence in response to the first. As with stage two, the actors remain frozen but play with their sentences. Repeating the process outlined in stage 2.

Follow with a discussion. Look carefully at how words change meaning and interpretation.

Stage 4: The process of stage 1 is repeated with the image and, as with stage 3 the first actor enters with a sentence. However now as the others complete the image the sentences become a conversation. The actors remain still but the discussion develops. Allow this conversation to develop over 10-15 minutes, over time this can expand but actors need to become accustomed to being frozen and the discomfort that comes with this. The conversation will develop beyond the script and new ideas will be explored.

Follow with a discussion about:

- the limits of staying frozen but also the freedom that comes with it
- the use of language and how it has developed over the stages
- the new information that came from the exercise: what have you learned about the character, their situation etc.
- how your ideas and preconceptions about the play have altered.

Stage 5: Repeat all of stage 4 but now introduce movement.

Discuss the following:

- how the different stages have altered pint of view, meaning and so on
- our focus on language & the power of image
- the importance of how we use words and the need to strip them back at times to understand the bigger picture and reconnect with our characters.

Me myself and I

Working silently in groups of three. One person moulds the other two to represent two contrasting views of his character; how he views himself and how he believes he is viewed by others. He does not tell the statues which version of him they represent. When the sculptor is happy with his work, he approaches each statue and speaks to them, providing them with three words he feels describes each and then moves to stand behind the two statues. The statues are now armed with two pieces of information: the shape they have been moulded into and the three words allocated them. They now come to life to create a monologue about who they are although physically they remain unable to move their bodies. This continues for approximately five minutes. The time can increase as actors become more accustomed to these styles of exercises.

When the monologue section is complete, the sculptor stands with his back to the statues so that all three have their backs to one another. He places himself in a position representative of how he desires to be and be seen. There are now three statues, how the sculptor views himself (the character), how he believes others see him, and his 'ideal'. The sculptor proceeds, still with his back to the other two statues, to describe the changes he would need to make to himself and in his life to achieve his ideal. If convinced by what they hear, each statue moves a little to represent how that change would affect their position. When the sculptor finishes speaking, the three statues turn to face one another and compare their similarities and differences through discussion. However each argues their perspective and they must try to convince one another which has the 'correct' view. By so doing they must also explain why they reject certain ideas.

Significant ages

Divide into groups of 5 to 7. One person in each group stands apart from the others who form a line. He thinks of significant periods in his character's life, noting the age he was each time. He then moulds the others into statues representative of himself at each of the ages he has chosen. With this complete, the protagonist passes from one to the other speaking to them, offering advice, warnings, encouragement, whatever is relevant to the age and the event that marked that period of his life. The statues stay frozen and unresponsive throughout.

After the protagonist has spoken to the statues individually, they can begin to ask questions, request further clarification or even challenge him but they cannot move. Now they can speak, all the statues are free to talk at the same time so their job is to get the attention of the protagonist. This process is repeated for each individual. However the statues can only behave according to the age that they were given and therefore can only discuss with the mindset of that age.

Time should be given to the group afterwards, during which they can discuss which age each was most drawn to and why, which they wanted to avoid, which surprised them. This exercise can be repeated not only for the characters in the play, but also for those who are implied. For example in The Art of Silence we have Emilio, but we also have the torturer, other prisoners, the prison guards, the doctor, Emilio's wife etc.

The Sin Eater

The Sin Eater

The play has been written for two characters – the torturer and the interviewer. However it is important to note that the torturer covers a number of different stories from various torturers. It is not intended to be the voice of one person. The play could therefore have various actors playing the torturer, or one single actor.

The scenery consists of two chairs and a table with a simple cloth, a jug of water and two glasses. Single spotlights are used throughout to mark the positions of the chairs, and general lights on the stage area. No other lighting is used and the starkness of the stage and lack of backdrop is essential.

The play centres on memories of interviews and material from interviews – some (semi) fabricated, the majority factual. The factual accounts have not been attributed and the torturer remains nameless deliberately to emphasise how it could be any one of us, that his monstrous capacity does not give him a monstrous appearance and that he could easily be the person standing next to us waiting for the bus, sitting next to us in a café, a neighbour, someone we work with, even a member of our own family.

Spotlight comes up stage right. Torturer has his head hidden in his hands, interviewer circles him asking his questions but the other shows no acknowledgement.

Interviewer What makes a man a monster? What makes him act in that way? How does he sleep at night? How does he go home to his family and talk about his day? Tell me, what makes a man a monster? *(lights fade)*

Torturer *(standing with his back to the audience leaning against a chair)* When people talk of torture all they imagine is the victim – what they must have gone through, how they suffered. Then they talk of the monsters that carried out the torture, what animals they must be, how they lack any sense of humanity, of decency, that they are the stuff nightmares are made of. *(Pauses then turns to the audience, hands resting on the back of the chair)* But you could be the monster of that nightmare just as easily as you could be the victim. And when the truth is told I, the torturer, I too am a victim ... I was just following orders.

Interviewer *(spotlight comes up stage left, interviewer is seated on the chair head in hands. Speaks with controlled anger)* How often I heard that throughout the interviews! *(sarcastically)* Just following orders! How often I despised them with all my judgmental self-righteousness. I began the interviews with hate, I hated them for what they had done, I couldn't understand what would ever make one man do that to another. How I despised them. I attacked them in the interviews no matter how hard I tried not to, I judged them for every act, every word *(long pause)*...at least in the beginning ... in the beginning it was like that ... then I stopped hating them, stopped judging them *(pause)* and that was when it got even harder. It is so much easier to hate.

Torturer *(taking a seat and speaking matter of fact)* I have a well-adjusted personality. I seem to live a normal life. Who would ever have guessed? Not even my family knew. My wife never imagined that the loving husband who slept by her side was an inhumane monster; my children never knew that their doting father was the monster of their imaginations. *(laughs then stops suddenly, silence)*

Interviewer *(remembering, uncomfortable and shifting around on the seat)* But the problem is that nothing is ever black and white – some were animals and I faced them with disgust, horror ... even fear at times, as I realised there were no depths these people would not sink to under the justification of following orders. But others were simply 'normal' people *(looks incredulously at audience)* – they did not come across as inhumane, uncivilised, sadistic. Just normal people. *(spoken with dismay, pauses before continuing looking directly at the audience)* Just like you and me. People that could have been me. *(pause)* And that felt so unfair, so difficult for my mind to accept.

Torturer I am two people. *(definitively)* The one who tortured has been dead a long time. I will not resurrect him; it is not who I am. So take your questions somewhere else and let me be. I've made my peace.

Interviewer *(spoken to the audience but directed at the torturer)* Is it yours to make? How do we differentiate between what we were and what we are? *(torturer and interviewer look directly at one another)* Can we really leave the past behind, especially when it has left us with blood on our hands?

Torturer *(interviewer and torturer face one another for the first time)* Did you come to interview me or to condemn me? I know what I did, you don't need to relate it to me. Do you get pleasure in doing that? Is it the details you want so badly, you sanctimonious bastard! We all have blood on our hands my friend, every one of us…some of us just believe we can wash it away *(laughs to himself)*.

Interviewer I would sit in the interviews going over supermarket lists in my head, or things I needed to do – anything to block out what I was hearing, to bring in everything that was ordinary and necessary in my own life. I was terrified that if I listened to the details too much, paid too much attention it would get in my head…and I would never be able to get it out.

Torturer *(mockingly)* Being a torturer is not infectious. *(laughing)*

Interviewer But evil is contagious.

Torturer	Perhaps – fear certainly is. Are you afraid my friend?
Interviewer	I am not your friend.
Torturer	*(in a manipulating manner)* Strange how you respond to the notion of our friendship and not that of your fear.
Interviewer	Aren't we all afraid ... of something ... of fear itself.
Torturer	*(as he speaks he moves towards the interviewer in a mocking way sniffing around him. They never look at one another and in the final words the torturer moves towards the interviewer's ear and whispers audibly)* You have a lot to learn my friend. Fear smells like a rotting carcass and a skilful torturer sniffs it out and moves in for the kill. *(walks back to his seat laughing, speaking generally and not aimed at anyone in particular)* We all have blood on our hands – every single one of us.
Interviewer	I've asked myself so many times – then, even now, perhaps more so now – *(looking down at his hands and speaking to them)* I look at my own hands. Do I have blood on my hands because I listened to him, to all of them? Because I ... because I stopped hating them, some of them, for what they had done? *(looking up towards audience)* Do I have blood on my hands for all the times I've stayed silent, not spoken out, not acted? I just don't know anymore. Things used to be clearer – before all this I mean – before I listened to the stories, all the stories, the

Torturer	torturers, the ones who were tortured, their families ... Sometimes I don't even know when their story ends and mine begins. *(playing mind games with the interviewer)* It's strange isn't it how someone else's story gets entwined with your own. People you would never have imagined you had anything in common with, never imagined that your paths would ever cross. *(change in tone as the torturer moves from playing with the interviewer to realising that this also relates to his own relationship with those he tortured)* Then something happens and suddenly it's all tied together and no matter what you do you can't free yourself. How do you free yourself from someone else's story when you've become a part of it – without meaning to... People talk about how the victims build this relationship with the torturer, loving them because they are the ones with the power to stop their suffering. It's strange but no one ever talks about how we need them, that those moments of love make us less evil in our own eyes and minds...
Interviewer	...you mean they give a justification for your existence.
Torturer	We all love to feel needed. *(Changing tact)* After all that's why you're here?
Interviewer	Go to hell.
Torturer	I make you feel good about yourself. You need me as much as I need you.

Interviewer	Bread, eggs, coffee, milk. Lists over and over. Block it out. Don't think. That's what he wants. Don't react. Don't let him in your head. *(thinking aloud, while the following seem to be a response to one another, there is no sense of contact or acknowledgement between them)* So what makes a man become a torturer?
Torturer	We did what we did to save our people, to protect them. A few small sacrifices for a greater good!
Interviewer	*(weighing up what has been said, cynicism coming through)* A few *small* sacrifices he said, as if they weren't even real people, insignificant numbers. Wearing the mask of protection, the protection of a state. He weighs the value of one life and favours the lives of thousands. He portends to defend with his acts of torture. *(long pause)* A clever justification – the patriot seems not to be so perverse in his acts ... at least, not on the surface
Torturer	Just following orders! I was not the one responsible.
Interviewer	*(angrily)* No! No! There has to be more to it than that. I could never accept that it could be that simple. *(spoken quietly, with a sense of resignation)* What frightened me was that in so many cases it actually was ...
Torturer	Our training made it seem routine. When the horror is removed it simply becomes a job. A job like any other. *(laughs)* I never thought I could do otherwise. And there was

	a mentality that – that the people we were in charge of, well, that they were not humans.
Interviewer	*(thinking, remembering)* And my training? It hadn't covered this ... any of this. *(refocusing)* Ordinary people doing 'ordinary' jobs – no sense of hostility. It was rarely personal they told me. In a strange way the stories became addictive. I wanted to hear more and more, more details. It was a way to try to understand. *(pause)* It was a way to punish myself. *(long silence)* Need to phone the dentist. Go to the shops. Meet friends... Need to make lists, lists after lists, think of anything but this.
Torturer	*(standing defiantly)* I am a victim too! They made me do it. They lied to me. I was given the orders what else could I do? You call me a coward but...
Interviewer	Sometimes I no longer know what being a coward means. Aren't we all cowards in one way or another? Am I not a coward? I often think that I am. I sit there with my tape recorder, pen and paper in hand, and use it as the wall to keep me out of the world I investigate, scared of what would happen if I didn't have those tools to protect me. It was the same interviewing the ones who had been tortured ... We are all always running away from something, something inside of us, something that strikes an all too familiar chord ... something that makes the line between us and them fade ... *(looking directly at the audience)* After the first interview I went home and threw up, I

showered and showered, afraid I think that somehow I had been contaminated, afraid that I was tainted by what I had heard, dirty, afraid that things would never be the same. They never were. *(long pause)* After the second interview I came home and cried, I cried for everything, for everyone I had ever loved who had died, for childhood memories, for a purity of life that could never now be mine. We can never unhear what we have heard…no matter how hard we try. *(long pause, looking directly at the audience)* After the third interview I was numb, I felt nothing. *(long pause then speaks directly to the audience)* You know people always ask me about the interviews and the work but you know you can never share it, that they don't want to hear *that*! And I don't blame them but how do I explain the person I have become because of it – the good *and* the bad. How do I explain what makes me seem so cold at times, so distant, so hard? How do I explain the place beyond hatred, beyond fear, beyond every nightmare that it sent me to? The nightmare I never imagined I would be able to scrape my way back from. They judge me from the outside – they don't try to understand because they don't want to – my reality would upset theirs far, far too much. *(pause)* Torture can take many forms and sometimes the worst can be what we do to ourselves *(head in hands)*.

Torturer   You know my children grew up thinking that we had moved to another country, that we'd had to flee our native land, because I was a political exile ... because I had been tortured. It wasn't that I had told them that ... they just assumed ... and it was easier ... we never spoke of it, they just thought it was too hard for me to talk about it. They were right – it was too hard, far too hard to talk about it. I mean how do you tell your own children that the man they thought was a hero is really the monster, the torturer not the victim. *(long pause)* Then they found out. They looked at me with such hatred and disgust, as if they didn't know me ... they still do. *(stifles emotion as he breaks down)*

Interviewer Didn't you try to explain?

Torturer Of course I did! At first. But explain what? How could I explain? How could I excuse my actions to them? How do I make it up to them for living a lie? One moment I was their hero, the next they despised me. Those looks of disgust, of hate – I know those looks, trust me, I know those looks so well.

Interviewer The looks you see even when you close your eyes. My friend I think I know them too. The reflection that looks back at you every day.

Torturer *(starts to tell jokes about people being tortured – a series of sick and distasteful jokes and laughs at them – the actors should source jokes relevant to where the play is being performed)*

Interviewer There was one in particular, the first time I tried to talk to him all he did was tell jokes. At first I was confused...the jokes...so

	inappropriate, sick...like he was goading me for a reaction.
Torturer	They say that some personalities are more capable ... the psychologists, psychiatrists ... that's what they say ... looking for a plausible reason to help us all sleep better at night. *(speaks directly to the audience)* But there's no real difference between us – geography, politics, religion, language ... but at the end of the day, you and me, we're the same. Situation ... that's what made me what I was *(looks at interviewer)* ...
Interviewer	*(refusing to accept, trying to block out what he is hearing)* No! I have to believe that there is more to it than that! What makes that ordinary person the demon of our imaginations?
Torturer	*(with increasing anger)* Ideology? Indoctrination? Class? Intelligence? Training? Society? Situation? A predisposition to torture? Which one sits better with *your* conscience? *(laughs)*
Interviewer	How do you – how does 'one' - become a torturer? I mean do they look for certain skills...
Torturer	*(laughing)* You mean do we put it on our curriculum vitae?
Interviewer	But how do they pick you out – how do they know you will do it, that you are ...
Torturer	...capable of such evil? Sufficiently depraved? There are different kinds of torturers – the ones who sit in an office and give the orders, they are the experts.

Interviewer The ones who wash their hands ... the ones with no visible stains.

Torturer The thing is that they are good, very good. They know how to get people to do what they want. They sense it in some, the need for power, control...others they work on fear, they tell you they will get your family, that they will do it to you if you don't... you think I'll do it for a little while till I find a way out but then you wake up one morning and you've been doing it for years and it's all you know... and it's too late you can't get out.

Interviewer *(with a sense of recognition for his own situation)* You know too much.

Torturer You feel too little. *(pause)* Part of you doesn't want out. Where would you go – both sides hate you. What would you do? You've become the necessary evil.

Interviewer Necessary?

Torturer My friend don't be so naïve, people like me are needed everywhere. *(smiling)* And so are people like you.

Interviewer What skills does a torturer have?

Torturer Efficient. Organised.

Interviewer Hateful!

Torturer How dramatic! Hate has nothing to do with it. It never did.

Interviewer Indifferent

Torturer	Indifferent to what? To the individual – perhaps. To the job – never. We always took a certain pride in what we did.
Interviewer	Pride!
Torturer	Creative ... artistic ... these are not random acts, it is a process, an art in itself.
Interviewer	A process of destruction . . .
Torturer	... of mastery!
Interviewer	I'd go home and people would ask 'how was your day?' What do you say? Fine? I hate that word. I hate all that it truly came to mean. Fine ended the conversation before it could begin, fine hid the truth of what was in my head. Fine dismissed the nightmares and the anger. Fine was everything I wasn't and never would be again. *(Torturer starts once again to tell jokes about people being tortured – a series of sick and distasteful jokes and laughs at them)* The second time I listened to his jokes I laughed. I laughed! *(pause)* God help me.
Torturer	In different circumstances, you and me, we would have been friends.
Interviewer	No. Never. Yes. Probably. God help me. How do I know? How can I ever know if the person who served me in the supermarket, the friend I grew up with, the person I passed in the street, how do I know if they are... how do I know where the monsters are when they look and act like me? Oh God. How do I know I am not one of them? *(desperate, upset and then slowly coming to an awareness and amused by the irony)* So this

	is what a torturer does – find a way inside my head, destroy me from within.
Torturer	*(whispering in the ear of the interviewer)* So much more effective than the beatings and the broken bones. They can mend.
Interviewer	*(returning to interview situation)* Few of them claimed to have had any anger at the time, there was no vindictiveness, no hatred...
Torturer	*(eager to explain)* Torture brutalises the torturer ... dehumanises us even further ...
Interviewer	*(sarcastically)* ... did it make you more mindless, more obedient?
Torturer	*(matter of fact)* I couldn't bring myself to disobey. The orders came from above, we were just following orders. We all end up isolated, strangers to others *(pause)*, strangers even to ourselves. At first it was a belief that we were superior, the elite. Then, when the 'climate of fear' had passed we were outcasts, the scapegoats ... the cancerous tumour that you all want to pretend does not exist. *(facing the interviewer angrily)* Well we do exist ... and we always will! *(mockingly, walks up to interviewer and pokes him in the head menacingly)* Even if it's just inside your head! *(they both stop and look at each other, torturer laughs, interviewer starts to laugh too and then they stop dead and turn away from one another).*
Interviewer	Some cried as they spoke to me. Some it seemed wanted pity, wanted me to see them

as the victim in it all ... but some, just some, cried from shame and guilt. And that was worse, that made me more uncomfortable – if the monsters came across as monsters with no feelings or emotions, no sense of guilt, then it was easy to see them as apart from me and my world, easy to remain untainted. I was once told that the art of the interviewer was to listen yet know when not to hear, to talk without ever speaking. And so I listened in silence and each night after the interviews I tried to teach myself slowly how to unhear all that had been said ... but that is a process that never ends ... you remember ... things that were said, things that happened... you remember when you least expect it ... it comes back with no warning ... and you are left with the memories and the inability to tell anyone ... to explain ... the inability to speak of the unspeakable ... and you, like *them*, just like *them*, remain in your own world of silence and secrets.

Torturer Few people know how loud silence can be. When you hear those screams, begging for their lives, their pain and then you go home and you can't stop listening to the silence all around you. Every sound pierces your ears. *(uncomfortable remembrance)* We always placed a hood on their heads. That was the protocol, they said it was to disorientate the victim, make them lose any sense of reality, and to make sure they never saw our faces. But you know I think the hood was for us, it helped us never see them as people, individuals – our crimes were faceless and, in that way, they could not be counted. I read once that serial killers often cover the face of their victims to dehumanise them – the focus then is on the act and not the individual. I felt sick when I read that, when I realised ... After the torture I tried to look after them, get them some extra food, clean water, even cigarettes. I wanted them to like me.

Interviewer Wanted or needed?

Torturer I wanted to let them know it wasn't personal. This was my job that was all. We only wanted information off them – we weren't punishing them. *(long pause)* Often I think that one day I will go back and look for them all and their families and tell them how sorry I am. I imagine it sometimes, what it would be like, how they might react I imagine what I might say to them, where would I begin to explain ... I know they must hate me ... I know that ... I understand that *(long pause)*. But I know that I will never go back. How can I? That's not cowardice, that's reality. You have to learn to live with the hate. You have to find a way to live with what you did...or what you didn't do...*(smiling at the interviewer)* You and me both my friend.

Interviewer It's a matter of conscience. *(torturer laughs loudly)*

Torturer *(turning to face the interviewer in fury)* And what would *you* know about that?

Interviewer And what did I know? Although now I sometimes think I know too much and I have learned that our conscience plays tricks on us – I carried the guilt of those who were tortured and survived ... now I carry the guilt of the torturers and the guilt of those who did nothing. I carry the guilt for crimes I did not commit. I am no different although I like to tell myself I am. How else can I sleep at night?

Torturer *(starts once again to tell jokes about people being tortured – a series of sick and distasteful jokes and laughs at them)*

Interviewer *(tells a joke about people being tortured – both the torture and the interview laugh loudly, then stop. Silence.)*

Torturer I wonder when this will all ever end. First all you care about is getting away – not being the scapegoat. You pray that nobody will recognise you in the street, point you out – tell everyone what you did. Even when you run to another country you are looking over your shoulder all the time, knowing that one day someone might recognise you. And if that fear ever lessens, it's in those moments that the guilt creeps in. *(pause)* Does death remove the guilt?

Interviewer I don't know.

Both *(quietly)* I hope so.

Interviewer I stumbled thinking of questions, what to ask next, not knowing what to ask, what to say to them. Months later when I listened to the cassettes of the interviews I cringed at my own naivety, my stupidity. I no longer recognised the person asking the questions – I didn't know him anymore. I didn't want to ... but I didn't want to know the person it had all made me either. *(turns to the torturer)* How do you *(correcting himself obviously in an attempt not to be so subjective)* ... how does a torturer hold on to a positive self-image?

Torturer *(laughs at the stupidity of the question replies sarcastically)* Positive reinforcement – we provide a service with many happy customers, we have a largely satisfied society. *(laughs)*

Interviewer *(change in tempo, return to the interview set up)* Did you feel an empathy with the ones you tortured, concern for them?

Torturer *(furiously)* Concern for *them*? You want me to feel pity for *them*? Why? They brought this on themselves. It was me I felt sorry for! Me! I was the one posted there, I was the one with the shit job! Who felt sorry for me? And no matter what I did, others were doing worse . . .

Interviewer They always told me of someone else who had been more inhumane, more monstrous. They were always eager to tell me about the others as if by so doing they painted themselves in a better light. *(pause)* And so many of them blamed the ones they had had to torture, saw their own dehumanization as having been their fault and that somehow that made them the injured party, the true victim in all of this. I learned not to try and rationalise this with them ... I tried at first . . but we came from different worlds and the truth is not always clear ... Truth! *(laughs)* What is truth anyway? Everyone's truth is different. Can one person's truth be truer than another's?

Torturer *(mockingly)* If you cannot find the truth right where you are, where else do you expect to find it?

Interviewer *(frustrated)* Lying is the simplest form of self-defence.

Torturer They say that the ability to ask questions is the greatest resource in learning the truth. *(sarcastically)* Maybe you need to work on your interview technique.

Interviewer *(a mixture of sarcasm and anger)* I'm learning to never assume the obvious is true. *(pause)* One victim told me how they kept him for eight months and how the worst part was listening to the screams of others as they were tortured. For eight months he heard those screams day and night.

Torturer It was my job for twelve years – torturing them. For twelve years I heard those screams day and night. You cannot ever imagine what that was like. Listen to that and then try and live a normal life! Go home at night to your family after listening to those screams hour after hour, pretending that you have had a normal day, that you live a normal life...And I still hear the screams, they never go away, *(getting desperate)* and I wake up at night sometimes and I realise

	that those screams, those screams I hear, they are my own!
Interviewer	Torture had destroyed the lives of all of them – torturer or tortured.
Torturer	Nothing can ever be the same. I don't expect forgiveness. I don't want pity.
Interviewer	Then what do you want?
Torturer	To sleep at night. To sleep a whole night without the nightmares, the memories, to believe that who I was is no longer who I am, to change what I cannot change … to sleep and never wake up.
Interviewer	And so the torturer ends up torturing himself *(laughs)*
Torturer	Does the irony please you? Does it entertain you? Remember you too are part of the nightmare now my friend! How do you sleep at night? So tell me, what do you want?
Interviewer	*(Looking away, speaking to himself)* Sometimes, just sometimes I realise I long for the same – a night of uninterrupted sleep, for the memories to fade, to believe I am other than I am, to change what I cannot change, to never have heard what I have heard … to sleep… to sleep and never wake up.
Torturer	Many just wanted to die – to end it all. The pain was what broke them, but we broke them faster if they couldn't breathe – that will make any man desperate – the baths, 'submarino' we called it. Then they begged

and cried and gave us names – any names – told us anything they thought we wanted to hear. The information was useless, we knew that. They would have said anything to make us stop. But it wasn't about the names. You knew after when they were back in the cell, knowing what they had done, that's when you knew you had them ... broken. The information became less and less significant ...

Interviewer *(pacing, restless)* The lesson: words are useless. Nothing can stop the torture. *(pause)* Nothing. And that was what stayed with me, what stays with me now. How can I explain that to you? One interview contradicted another. They even contradicted themselves as they spoke to me. Many refused to let me record the interviews, only allowing me to take notes. Most didn't trust me and I couldn't blame them, because I never trusted them.

Torturer *(change in tempo)* Is the intentional infliction of extreme *mental* suffering on a non-consenting, defenceless person necessarily torture?

Interviewer Searing with hot irons, burning at the stake, electric shock treatment to the genitals, the anus, cutting out parts of the body, the tongue, entrails or genitals, severe beatings, suspending by the legs with arms tied behind back, applying thumbscrews, inserting a needle under the fingernails, drilling through an unanesthetized tooth, making a person crouch for hours in the 'Z'

	position, waterboarding - continuously immersing the head in water until close to point of drowning - denying food, water or sleep for days or weeks or months on end ... breaking a person's will is short of entirely destroying or subsuming their autonomy ... *(getting angry)* So I don't know! Why don't you tell me! Is the intentional infliction of extreme *mental* suffering on a non-consenting, defenceless person necessarily torture?
Torturer	Of course I knew it was wrong. We all did. On one level at least ... but sometimes they just got to you, the ones who wouldn't crack and it became like a kind of mission to see how long it would take to crack them, to see what it would take. Some of the bastards never cracked but you know we got inside their head one way or another, those bastards are fucked for life now. And so are we.
Interviewer	Make my list. Don't think. Don't process what they say. Lists. Meet friends at 7pm. Go to restaurant. Have dinner. Make jokes. Laugh. Go for a drink. Go home. Go to bed. Cry. Make a list for the next day ... and the next ... and the next ... lists not to forget ... lists not to think ... lists not to hear. *(long pause)* So why, why did they do what they had done? I truly wanted to try to understand but something made it impossible.
Torturer	*(smiling sarcastically)* Perhaps it's your humanity.

Interviewer	And some related what they had done with pride and satisfaction.
Torturer	I attached wires to their genitals and shocked them with electricity, once I even tore off a man's testicles with a rope. They knew everything we were doing. They saw what condition the victims were in - their marks and bruises. They didn't do anything. There were many who were not in agreement, but they couldn't get out ... if we wanted to leave, we would have to have left dead. I was an interrogator *not* a torturer! But sometimes physical torture is necessary in an interrogation.
Interviewer	Others who knew him told me that sometimes he killed because he was ordered to, other times, because he wanted to.
Torturer	I didn't do it because I liked it, nor because I had ideas from the far right... I never considered myself an ultra right-wing person or a leftist. ... here, if someone comes and offers you a high salary, of course you're going to accept... you'd have done the same...
Interviewer	They all had their reasons.
Torturer	I was involved. Yes, I participated. Yes, I was involved with torture. I was doing a job, something I did to put food on the table for my children. I knew it wasn't right. But if I get an order and I oppose, I'm risking my life. So what could I do? *(shrugging his shoulders)* I never wanted to wash my hands of what I did. I know I have responsibility. I

knew what I was doing. But there is a point where you go through this door and you cannot go back out through that same door, never.

Interviewer Another told me...

Torturer I did it to earn merit. I was from a poor family, it was a way to work up the ranks. I hogtied and kicked them, pulled the hair off their legs, jolted their bodies with electricity and smothered them with a rubber hood. If that failed I threatened to harm their families, I'd tell them it's better you cooperate, because if you don't, we're going to bring them in and rape them and torture them and kill them. We would show them photos of their family. We would say, 'We're going to get your mother and rape her in front of you.' Then we would make it seem like we went to get the mother. That would get them going! *(laughs)* I thought the doors to my future were open. *(long pause)* I was wrong. And what you have seen, what you have done, you have to take to your grave, you reach that point when ... when you have no choice.

Interviewer And me? What I have heard, I have to take to my grave, I have no choice. *(pause)* It all seemed so senseless, so futile ... them, what they had done, and now me sitting there, listening. I didn't even know why anymore. I think I just wanted to or needed to try to understand. I had been working with torture victims for so long, I had heard so many stories and I needed to understand how one man could do this to another. I needed to believe that they were abnormal beings, monsters or demons. I needed to make sense of it all in my own head. But I went looking for answers that didn't exist.

Torturer Perhaps what you try so hard to understand, the answers you seek, perhaps they are inside of you. You didn't need to seek me out. I can't help you sleep more easily at night. How can I? I can't even help myself.

Interviewer Is torture ever justified? I think it is better sometimes to never begin a search for meaning because if you do you have to finish it, no matter what happens. *(long pause)* Insomnia. Anti-social. Prone to rage and fighting. Suicidal. Nightmares. It was strange but the list was practically identical to their victims. Years on they both suffered. And while part of me felt some pleasure that the torturers suffered, the irony was almost overwhelming.

Torturer Doing what is appropriate may not always be what is right. That's just how it is.

Interviewer Those words echo in my head and I wonder sometimes what are we really capable of? Some had acted honourably since – risked everything and become outcasts by speaking out and some I felt a certain respect for and that in itself terrified me.

Torturer You don't need to seek people 'like me' out in the far corners of the earth, look around you, your own people, your leaders ... *(taunting)* look at yourself.

Interviewer	*(indignant and scared)* I'm not you, I'm not like you!
Torturer	How do you know, but for a twist of fate you might just have been . . .
Interviewer	He laughed and laughed. I wanted to run out or shout at him, I wanted to grab him, shake him and tell him I would never be like him. And then I realised that was what he wanted, he was provoking me, he wanted me to get angry, he wanted me to show my own predilection to torture. After that interview I stopped for a while. I needed time to process all that was happening around me, all that was in my head. I needed time to reassure myself I was different from these monsters. But was I? They weren't all monsters and the ones who behaved without humanity, it was easy to differentiate myself from them ... but the others . . .
Torturer	So many of us have an inability to understand the suffering of another human being and *that* is a prerequisite to inflicting torture.
Interviewer	When they said those things, I wanted to dismiss them, believe they were untrue.
Torturer	Is it worse to torture someone than to kill them?
Interviewer	What?
Torturer	Which is worse? Come on – answer!
Interviewer	Torture!
Torturer	Torture is worse than murder! And you think my ethics are dubious! *(laughs)*

	Torture does not necessarily involve killing, let alone murder. The duration of the torture might be brief, one's will might not ultimately be broken, and one might go on to live a long and happy life…
Interviewer	Killing is an infringement of the right to life and the right to autonomy. Torture is an infringement of the right to autonomy ...
Torturer	... but not necessarily of the right to life.
Interviewer	Maybe torturers are simply less admirable than murderers! We looked at one another and both laughed. I don't know why I laughed. Pain is worse in a way that ending a life is not. They would have preferred death you know.
Torturer	You know nothing! Only some would have preferred death, others were piss scared and begged us to let them live. Cried like little children and pissed and shat in their pants. How does that sit with your idealistic notions of bravery?
Interviewer	At least murderers aren't such cowards! They don't hide behind some authority figure as an excuse for their depravity. *(speaking aside)* I didn't even know what I was saying, everything was building up. I hated him, hated him for making me think of things I didn't want to think about, for putting things in my head that wouldn't leave. I couldn't think straight. I couldn't clear my own head. *(gripping sides of head)*
Torturer	Get out! Get out!

Interviewer	*(both interviewer and torturer act this out as the interviewer speaks)* He had had a glass of water in his hand and he threw it at the wall smashing it and then, with a force I never imagined an old man could have, he grabbed me by my arm and threw me out of his house and slammed the door. I stood outside for a moment pleased with myself that I had made him snap, that I had made him show a glimpse of the monster he had been and clearly still was. Then I started to shake and felt overwhelmed with sadness and shock at myself, at my reaction. Were we really any different? *(pause)* I just needed to clear my head, to think straight. I thought if I just had time to think, to sort all this out in my head, it would all be okay, it would all make sense ...
Torturer	*(in an attempt to justify himself)* You don't understand now, today ... I mean the purpose of torture is not as clear-cut as it was in the late 60s or 70s.
Interviewer	There was always a reason, an excuse, always somebody worse ... what does torture actually mean to you?
Torturer	That extra effort to inflict pain on...
Interviewer	...on someone already under your control!
Torturer	The purpose was to obtain a confession...
Interviewer	...an absurdly meaningless confession!
Torturer	The purpose was to obtain information...
Interviewer	...false and unreliable information
Torturer	The purpose was to punish...

Interviewer	…to instil fear!
Torturer	It was necessary!
Interviewer	And fill them with righteous hate?
Torturer	*(laughing)* A very self-righteous comment! Some of us did it because we *could*, because we were good at it. Torture is an art form; it takes skill and presence of mind. I don't expect *you* to understand
Interviewer	I don't think I want to!
Torturer:	Elicit compliance and collaboration from people usually not even involved. We would torture them so that they would testify against suspected 'enemies' of the state, they would give us information. Then we would turn them loose back into their community and they would be rejected by their own, some would even be tortured or killed by their own people. Christ – you've got to love the irony! *(laughing)* But some, just some, were stubborn bastards. That was when it became personal – a personal mission to break that one. It was their own fault.
Interviewer	It was always the exceptions that caused the problems. And the innocent victims?
Torturer	Don't be fooled there were never any innocent 'victims' – infants, children, youth, adults – they were *all* guilty of something.
Interviewer	I needed to make sense of the reality, of the suffering I was witness to – the suffering I was feeling, hearing, seeing, thinking of and in a strange way experiencing. I felt my

	hands had been bloodied and I didn't know how to rid myself of that ... of that guilt ...You know they draw no attention to themselves. Nothing makes them stand out. They don't openly advertise their hate, their evil behaviour. The torturers walk among us.
Torturer	Look around you my friend, people like me, we are everywhere! *(pause)* Go look in the mirror!
Interviewer	I comforted myself with the belief that these things happened in a time before mine, that the world no longer functioned in that way. How naïve I was! After all torture never goes out of fashion – the geography might change, the rationale, the face of the torturer ... but the torture remains and under the auspices of democracy torture, it seems has become even more justifiable, if not necessary ... that is what they would have us believe.
Torturer	For the torturer the fear of publicity is great; the fear of torture is not.
Interviewer	I wondered why they agreed to talk to me, why they would be willing to tell me what they had done.
Torturer	Everyone needs to tell their story – to let it go – to pass it on …
Interviewer	... to pass it on! That's what torture victims had told me. Sometimes I think I should never have done the interviews. That some things are better left laid to rest.
Torturer	But we needed someone to listen.

Interviewer	Why me?
Torturer	All stories need to be told ... sooner or later ... and when that time comes a listener is chosen *(starts to laugh)* we all need a sin eater.
Interviewer	That's what they used to call me – the sin eater.
Torturer	As a shamanic tradition, a sin eater would be employed by the family of a deceased person to eat a last meal of bread and salt from the belly of the corpse as it lay in state. Through this ritual it was believed that the sins of the dead person would be absorbed and the deceased would have clear passage to the hereafter. The sin eater was given a few coins for his trouble, but other than that was avoided, literally 'like the plague' by the community who regarded him as sin-filled and unclean as a result of his work. That is why sin eaters usually lived at the edge of the village and children were warned away from them.
Interviewer	So who is the torturer and who the tortured? Where do we draw the lines?
Torturer	Where do you and I really differ my friend? The only difference between us is that you call your depravity 'democracy'! *(laughs)* It is hard to realise what you are, is it not?
Interviewer	*(to himself)* Yet it is harder to realise what you might become.
Torturer	We used to tell them - If you live through this, no one will believe you. No one will listen. No one will care. We said it to break

	them, but look around you, what we said was true!
Interviewer	I closed my eyes overwhelmed by the sense, the realisation, that I was reliving the nightmare.
Torturer	*(coming up to the interviewer and taunting him, interviewer looks ahead without acknowledging him but with an increasing look of despair)* What makes a man a monster? What makes him act in that way? How does he sleep at night? How does he go home to his family and talk of his day? What makes a man a monster? *(Interviewer buries his head in his hands while the torturer laughs. Lights fade.)*
Interviewer:	In the end aren't we all…
Both	… just following orders! *(Lights fade)*
Interviewer	Torture can take many forms and sometimes the worst can be what we do to ourselves *(head in hands)*.
Torturer	*(acted out as he speaks, when he finishes speaking, he lies down at the feet of the interviewer)*
	The manner was that when a corpse was brought out of the house and laid on the bier; a loaf of bread was brought out and delivered to the sin-eater over the corps, as also a mazer-bowl full of beer, which he was to drink up, and sixpence in money, in consideration whereof he took upon him all the sins of the defunct, and

freed him (or her)
from Walking after
they were dead'
(John Aubrey, 'Remains of Gentilism'. As torturer lies down like a corpse the lights fade to black out))

The End

Workshop Ideas

Below are discussion points and exercises that can help not only lead us to a better understanding of the play, but also of Applied Theatre and what it involves. In all Applied Theatre and Theatre of the Oppressed exercises, discussion is key. Always allow ample time for discussion after each exercise and explore what has happened.

Discussion questions

1. Discuss the stage elements of the play and what makes it Applied Theatre e.g. set, lights, props etc.
2. The concept of applied plays is not to take sides but simply to tell the story. How do our feelings about both the torturer and the interviewer change throughout and why?
3. Applied Theatre often plays with the idea of victim and perpetrator roles being interchangeable. Discuss how this happens in the play.
4. In what moments do you find yourself disliking or rejecting the interviewer? Explain.
5. What is the purpose of this play?
6. We are all guilty of something. Discuss.
7. The set is designed to make an audience feel entrapped. How do you think this is achieved?
8. It has been said that torture is an art form, designed not to kill an individual but to break their spirit and then return them to their society as a lesson to others. Discuss.
9. Discuss why you think the torturer(s) are willing to speak about what they did.
10. What feelings is the writer trying to evoke in the audience and why?

11. Explain the interviewer's guilt and fear at liking the torturer.
12. The interviewer states 'Aren't we all afraid ... of something ... of fear itself.' What do you think was meant by this statement?
13. The torturer refers to himself as 'the necessary evil'. Discuss what he means by this.
14. The torturer says that 'we all have blood on our hands'. What does he mean by that?
15. Do you believe that we all have 'the torturer' inside of us, that capacity to do such terrible acts of the situation pushed us to it? Discuss.
16. We all have a basic desire/need to be liked, even the torturer sought that from his victims. Discuss.
17. The torturer states, 'Doing what is appropriate may not always be what is right.' Looking at today's state of affairs in around the world, how might you apply this statement.
18. The play tells of specific time and regime but has overtones of many issues in our society today. Discuss.
19. It is normal for an Applied Theatre performance to have a discussion time with the audience after the play. Why do you think this is necessary?
20. It has been said that Applied Theatre plays with our emotion and our certainties. Discuss how the play achieves this.
21. Discuss the concept of a 'sin eater' as described in the play.

Applied Theatre Exercises

When doing these exercises it is important to remember that the different stages will often be carried out on different days and do not need to be done in succession. The exercises can be adapted and used for any of the plays.

Please note that in Applied Theatre time should *always* be allocated to discuss and process the exercises after they have been completed.

S/he said, but s/he meant

An exercise to look at perception in our use of words. The actors go through selected lines from the play and perform them to one another. They then repeat replacing the line – where relevant – with what they thought they actually meant. For example the torturer's line may be 'I was simply following orders' but what he was actually thinking is, 'I was terrified not to do as they told me and I hurt others from fear', or 'I am innocent and my superiors are the ones you should be accusing not me'. Allow this new dialogue to develop and explore where it may take the concepts and our understanding of the characters.

Afterwards discuss as a group

- what changed in our interpretation of the play
- what changed in how we view each of the characters
- why we often say things that are not what we mean or really want to say. In particular why the group think these two characters do this.

The Body Speaks

Stage 1: Set the stage with the table and two chairs. This exercise plays with concepts of authority and body language. The actors sit facing one another in silence. One moves their position slightly to assume the superior position. The second actor moves to try to take over the superior position. For example, one may lean forward with their elbows on the table staring at the other; the other may turn to the side ignoring him. At that point the first actor moves again and so on. It is like a game of cat and mouse with changeable roles. It is important that this happens seated and in silence. Each new movement should be held for about 30-60 seconds in order to fully understand the effect of another's body language upon us.

After doing this for some time, positions can be changed to

- one actor seated and the other standing (then swap)
- both actors standing.

Discuss the power of body language over words and how we can interpret so much about feeling and though from body language.

Stage 2: Repeat all of stage 1 but this time the actors are allowed to repeat a single word each time. The word must reflect how the positions are making them feel. For example words chosen might be - *stressed, uncomfortable, powerful, scared, inferior, superior, challenged, angry* and so on.

Discuss how the use of the word affects how we read body language. Do the words match the body language you were reading? Look at how we often use our bodies to hide what we are feeling.

Stage 3: Repeat all of stage 1 but introduce the repetition of a phrase now instead of a single word. For example, a phrase might be: 'I feel lost', 'I don't want to be judged', 'I'm terrified I could become you' and so on. With each movement the phrase changes for each but it is NOT a conversation. Rather it is a comment that reflects how each individual is feeling in the position they are now in.

Discuss the difficulty of putting words to feelings and how we often express ourselves poorly as a result. How much of what was said was influenced by the other's words and/or body language?

Stage 4: We return to image and now words. The actors sit as outlined in stage 1 but this time the first actor takes one position and the second actor mimics what he sees. The first actor watches and adjusts his body if he feels the second actor is different in his body language. The two continue adjusting over a period of time. As they are trying to mirror one another moves will be small. The focus is on the interpretation and the fact that we think we come across a certain way but are usually wrong. If at any point the actors stop moving because they think they are a mirror image, allow the exercise to continue as one will move unintentionally and the other must be alert to copy immediately. This exercise can be carried out seated and/or standing. It takes time and patience to get the best results.

Discuss how the actors felt doing the exercise and how it sharpens focus and self-awareness.

Angel/Devil (alternative version)

Stage 1: In character one of the actors begins talking about his feelings. An actor on either side, one supports what he is saying and is encouraging; the other is critical and attacking. They have no physical contact with the actor in the middle and must stay in their seats, so they must look for ways to make themselves heard. Allow 15-20 minutes for this stage.

Stage 2: Stage 1 is repeated but this time the actor in the middle (who is one of the characters) can get up and move around. He can try to get away from the other actors. There can be no physical contact but the actors can pursue him wherever he goes and maintain very close proximity. Remember NO contact. Allow 15-20 minutes for this stage.

Stage 3: The actor in the middle exits the scene and the two actors who were the angel/devil argue between themselves about which one is correct and why. Allow 15-20 minutes for this stage.

Stage 4: The actor playing the character returns to the scene and presents a new monologue influenced by what he has heard and seen develop throughout the other stages. Allow 15-20 minutes for this stage.

Stage 5: Discussion with the whole group afterwards looks at what has happened and the changes which have occurred throughout the different stages above. Look carefully at how words change meaning and interpretation.

Images of the past

When doing this exercise it is unlikely that you will get through more than one or two images if completing all stages and the discussion period. It is advised that the different stages of the exercise are repeated on various occasions to enable the group to look at different images. This is also a great rehearsal tool for building character. In the example below it is the character of the torturer doing the exercise, however all stages should be repeated for the interviewer also.

If using this exercise for a play with multiple characters, each stage should be completed for all of them. It is a key way to understand the perspective of characters and their relationship to the world around them. Images should also be extensive and not limited to actual scenes or events mentioned in the play. They can be extended to include scenes implied by the information provided us in the play.

Stage 1: In character the torturer creates images from his past. These images could include acts of torture, time with his family and so on. Other actors are used to create the image. No words are spoken and each person must be moulded (not told or shown what to do) as an essential part of the creative process. When he is happy with the image, he inserts himself as himself into the image.

Each image is held for a few minutes enabling everyone involved to gather their thoughts and feelings about their position, the perspective they have based on what they can see from their position and their relationship to others. They should pay specific attention to their body language. For example, where they are looking, the placement of their feet and hands, if their body is closed off or defensive, if they are isolated or blinkered.

After a few minutes allow the actors to relax briefly and shake it out, before taking the same positions once more. This time the sculptor (the interviewer) has an actor take his position to enable him to look at the image as a whole and the role that he plays in it. When placing the other actor in the image to replace him, he should ensure that the position is exactly as it was before.

The image is held for 3-5 minutes during which time the interviewer observes the image from the outside. He can walk around the image and situate himself alongside others in the image to get a feel for their position physically, mentally and emotionally. Discuss the exercise as a group.

Stage 2: Stage 1 is repeated but this time the actor gives each person in the image a word to describe them or what they are feeling/thinking. Finally he takes his place and gives himself a word. For the next few minutes the actors altogether repeat their words to themselves, experimenting with volume, pitch and tone. Discuss the exercise as a group.

Stage 3: Stage 2 is repeated. This time the actors must use their word (only the single word that they have been given) to create a dialogue among themselves. Each person is restricted by their inability to move and only being able to use the one word. Encourage a keen listening to tone and pitch to appreciate the intended meaning of the words each time they are spoken. Discuss the exercise as a group.

Stage 4: Stage 2 is repeated with the sculptor (the interviewer) remaining out of the image and another actor in his place. The interviewer goes up to each person in the image in turn and speaks to them, perhaps he is trying to explain or justify himself, perhaps angry and outraged. Whatever he wants to say he speaks to them without physical contact. The person he is speaking to must remain still but can respond throughout using the single word they were given in stage 3. They may repeat the word like a question, an answer, whisper, shout, whatever they feel is an appropriate response to what the torturer is saying.

When the torturer no longer wishes to talk to them (for whatever reason) he moves to the next. However he may return at any time and pick it up again. Allow sufficient time for this. Also remember the sculptor is free to move but the others in the image are not which will affect the dynamic of the relationship. The interviewer can talk to anybody in the image except for the actor who replaced image. Discuss the exercise as a group.

Stage 5: Everyone leaves the image except for the actor who has taken the place of the torturer. This actor remains alone frozen in the position he was given. The sculptor now approaches him and both converse. This conversation could include questioning, accusations, seeking to understand, but throughout the actor in the image cannot move while the sculptor may move around freely. Allow this to continue for some time. In this way the limits to the actor's movement will add to his interpretation of his emotional and mental state. Discuss the exercise as a group.

Stage 6: The actors return to the image and the torturer takes his position in the image. All around him the others in the image discuss what they think of their situation, the scene and the torturer. They cannot move but can discuss freely. The torturer can neither move nor speak. Discuss the exercise as a group.

Significant ages (variation)

The actor in character, for example the torturer, moulds two other actors into himself. One is who he was before the time period of the play. In this case this would have been in his active role as a torturer. The other is a much older version of himself in the future. Finally he moulds himself into the man he is in the play.

The three form a triangle with their images so that they can all see one another. They remain still but begin a conversation where each presents only as the man he is at that time with the knowledge and attitude/beliefs he would have at that time.

For example:

- *The active torturer may be proud of working for his government and see what he is doing as his job, or he may feel pressured into doing the job because his family is under threat etc. In the play there are various justifications the torturers provided so any of these could be chosen.*
- *The torturer from the play could be full of excuses, or he might feel justified, or he may feel angry that people judge him for what he did and be unrepentant, or he might be ashamed and full of inner turmoil and guilt.*

> - *The older torturer would be able to look back on all of his life and may see things differently with his fuller life experiences.*

After allowing the conversation to develop over a period of time, the three in silence amend their images to reflect how they now feel about themselves for the time period they represent. They then choose one word to describe themselves and share it with the others.

Discuss as a group, those involved in the exercise and those observing it. Does it change perspective of the character?

Remember the exercise can be repeated for any of the characters, and for anybody mentioned in the play though not necessarily present. For example, the exercise could be carried out for one of the torturers victims. In this case reflection could take place over his feelings towards the torturer and we can look at how another's story affects our development of the characters in the play.

'til death do us part

There is no remedy for love but to love more.
Henry David Thoreau

Introduction

An analysis of ten separate studies on the prevalence of domestic violence found consistent findings: one in four women experience domestic violence over their lifetimes and between six to ten percent of women suffer domestic violence in a given year (Council of Europe, 2002). Around the world, at least one in every three women has been beaten, coerced into sex or otherwise abused during her lifetime. Most often, the abuser is a member of her own family. Studies suggest that up to 10 million children witness some form of domestic violence annually. Every nine seconds in the US a woman is assaulted or beaten. Domestic violence is the leading cause of injury to women—more than car accidents, muggings, and rapes combined. Every day in the US, more than three women are murdered by their husbands or boyfriends. In the UK on average, two women a week are killed by a violent partner or ex-partner - this constitutes nearly 40% of all female homicide victims. (Povey, (ed.), 2005; Home Office, 1999; Department of Health, 2005.) We tend to think of domestic violence as hitting, slapping and beating, but it can also include emotional abuse as well as forced marriage and so-called 'honour crimes'.

An innovative production exploring conflict in relationship. The play explores domestic abuse and the different perceptions of those involved, based on actual testimonies and interviews, challenging expectations and judgement throughout. 'Til death do us part, as with all TVO plays was written from testimonies of those whose experiences are described. While some changes have been made the story follows true-life experiences and attempts to represent the perception of both involved in the tragic events that ensued. Described by audience members as: *'fantastic', 'brave and bold work', 'an unforgettable experience', 'an experience unlike any other I have ever had in a theatre', 'sensitive, accurate, disturbing and cathartic all at the same time', 'The most disturbing aspect is that the play is presented in a way that audience allegiance shifts all the time. That's a shock, you think you will clearly side with the 'victim' but it's really not that simple.'*

In 2012 TVO began a domestic abuse project. Like all our projects the goal was to explore behaviour and help people come to a better understanding of themselves and their situations. The project led to work in prisons, refuge centres and safe houses, secure children's homes, universities and colleges. We worked with both survivors and perpetrators and used as a springboard and focus for the workshops. The feedback we got from both the male perpetrators and the female survivors was insightful. So many of the perpetrators were themselves survivors of domestic abuse and were shocked to see themselves in the role of the aggressor. The women we worked with began to talk to one another in the workshop in a way they had been unable to before, sharing their experiences. The exercises that accompanied the play allowed them to explore their relationships and experiences in ways that allowed for new insight. Key workers with both the women and men reported in their feedback that behaviour had changed – individuals seemed more at ease with themselves, less aggressive and more willing to engage with others. The play was performed with talk back sessions for the public in theatres and other community spaces.

Eight years later the play continues to be performed regularly and in multiple countries. Many support groups have used it in conjunction with their programmes for victims of abuse. Equally workshops have been carried out in prison with perpetrators in conjunction with behavioural programmes. The response in all instances has been extremely positive, with much discussion promoted, engagement from many who would not engage in other exercises and/or groups.

While we are told Kerry and Paul are a married couple with three children in the play, details are left vague deliberately in order to allow for the casting to vary from a young, to middle-aged, to elderly couple. The rationale behind this is that domestic abuse can happen at any time in a relationship and at any age.

The setting of the play consists of two chairs poised at angles towards one another, a small coffee table next to Paul is optional. The single prop used is a bottle that Paul drinks out of throughout the play.

Lights up. When Kerry speaks, she regularly becomes distracted and her conversation is disjointed as she jumps from one idea to another. Kerry and Paul are speaking towards the audience as if directed dialogue at a single person. They do not acknowledge one another's presence most of the time, except when it moves into re-enacting a memory.

Kerry I loves a soup I do – something about it, makes me feel at home, safe. A nice vegetable soup, or a lentil one, specially in the winter, gives you a cosy feeling, you know? *(distracted pause, continues but agitated)* Valentine's day *(pauses)* well I just felt so damn angry that he had found somebody new, you know and I was thinking, not about him with somebody else *(defensive)* that doesn't bother me at all, so don't be thinking it does cause it doesn't *(to audience)*, she's welcome to him if you ask me, welcome to him I tell you.

Paul *(stabling an intimate rapport with the audience with his joking/sarcastic manner)* Here we go again. She just goes on and on. Sometimes I wish there was a volume button, like the TV remote, or a mute button, that'd be even better. Click and no more noise, shut her up in a second. Turn her off! Yeh *(nodding to the audience)* that'd be great wouldn't it – what an easy life I'd have then.

Kerry It's just that I know what she's got to look forward to and it isn't good believe you me, no it isn't good. It was the thought, well the thought that he was with somebody and I know exactly how he works. Oh yes I certainly do, I know better than anyone else – it would be all money, *my* money, and all show, fancy restaurants, flowers and you know, like, well like part of me wanted to stalk him on valentine's day to see if he really was with somebody else and if he was spending money, *my* money, on somebody else and here's me in this horrendous financial situation. Not stalk him in a bad way like, just follow him around you know. Then I thought what would I do if I saw him with somebody else anyway. That's the thing, I'd stand there like an idiot I would. I'd say nothing, hide, walk away *(pauses as she deals with a sense of disappointment in herself)*. I had all these thoughts. I suppose they're natural feelings *(looking at audience seeking agreement and a sense of approval)* you know what I mean, well of course you do, just natural feelings like anyone would get on Valentine's Day.

Paul She just couldn't let go … in her own way pulling me back every time. *(with a knowing look to the audience)* Toying with me *(nodding his head knowingly)* that's what I say. You know what these women are like.

Kerry Sometimes the wrong just felt right. I don't know *(confused)* I can only tell you what it feels like.

Paul I felt like I couldn't breathe, like I was suffocating.

Kerry People perceive my husband…

Paul   Ex-husband

Kerry   Well people perceive my husband, my ex-husband, as being a very quiet, well-spoken man. People who don't know him, they think he's this lovely, quietly spoken family man. Bloody hell they have no idea! *(pause)* My son, you know what he says, well what he always says is 'you'll either turn around and get him or he'll get you'. *(pauses pensively)* I think he might be right my son, I think he might be right.

Paul   *(sarcastically)* I suppose it's the old saying, nobody knows what goes on behind closed doors.

Kerry   They say, 'oh what a wonderful man he is, what a wonderful family man'. Can you believe it? Can you bloody well believe it?

Paul   *(very rational and calm, a sense of self-justification)* It was only her, I only ever lost it with her. You know she'd push and push and just leave me with no damn choice! You know what I mean? She knew what she was doing *(to audience directly)* don't let anyone tell you different. And it takes two you know, anyone who tells you different they don't know what they're talking about.

Kerry   They don't know the real man. They don't know the man I lived with all them years. *(raising her voice)* I'll never be the same again – never. *(distracted, trying to find her way back through her own thoughts)* I got a plant for my daughter in town today. Nice

	smell. *(pause)* Smell. *(pause)* Smell is important you know.
Paul	She destroyed everything – me, us, the family, everything I had worked for all our lives. *(getting angrier)* And everyone thinks *she's* the victim!
Kerry	'Nobody will ever love you like I love you.' That's what he used to tell me. Well let me tell you I wouldn't want to be loved like that ever again. It was all control. That's not love. He's hoping he can chip away at me and I'll give in and take him back. *(pauses as if contemplating the idea)* It's easy to say don't look back, but I'm human and you do look back and … and part of me wishes that I still had the happy times…
Paul	…I wonder sometimes, were there ever any happy times?
Both	I have to look forward. *(pause, said in very different tones with different implications)* But something keeps pulling me back.
Kerry	He just keeps chipping away though. It's the same story every time. He's fine for a while, then he starts drinking again and gets himself in trouble… he goes into prison to dry out … gets food and a place to kip down. He's been in and out of prison so many bloody times he might as well move in there. I'm telling you! I'm sure they've got a cell with his name on it, ready, waiting for him like! *(tone becomes angrier and more defensive)* He's an evil man and I know I shouldn't have stayed with him, I know that,

	I don't need you or anybody else telling me that *(pause)* but I loved him.
Paul	*(tapping at his head more and more violently as he goes on)* Nipping away at my head all the time. Not enough money for this, we need that, you drink too much, do this, do that. She just kept nipping away. Nothing was good enough. The drink was the only way to get her to shut the fuck up. Block her out, that constant fuckin' whining. Then the drink couldn't even block her out anymore. *(mocking)* 'Poor me, no one knows how hard it is for me, no one knows how hard my life is with you. No one knows what you're really like. I don't know why I stay.' Fuck! I don't know either you stupid bitch. Well there's the fuckin' door. That's what I say! Who the fuck's stopping you? *(to audience, incredulous)* People think I wouldn't let her leave, fuck I'd have packed her bags and carried them to the damn taxi. I wasn't stopping her, no way.
Kerry	I was going to see a psychiatrist. The Counsellor said it would be good for me, that it might help me make sense of things.
Paul	*(as if sharing a confidential piece of information with the audience)* She's mental she is.
Kerry	*(very defensive)* Not cos I'm mental. To offload, you understand. But it's the stigma you know, people might think I'm crazy *(defensively)* and I'm not. That's what he tells people, that I'm crazy and I'm not.

Paul	Crazy fuckin' bitch.

Kerry	He would always criticise me, my family and my friends, then he started on the children, I wasn't having none of that. No I was not. You've got to set lines you know, boundaries like, and you just don't cross them. He controlled all the money. He was always trying to put me down. Always trying to make me feel inferior to him. Always belittling me. He tried to keep me from my friends and soon, well soon they just stopped coming to the house. *(reminiscing)* But you know, you wouldn't think it now but well, when we got married it was…well… well I was…

Paul	*(reminiscing on his own feelings)* … so much in love.

Kerry	I just wanted to spend the rest of my life with this man – I was so, so deeply in love with him – I thought I'd die if I wasn't with him. And there was no aggression in him. Honest. Placid he was, very very placid and we were…

Paul	…happy.

Kerry	…in love.

Paul	I'm not happy now.

Kerry	I'm not sure I ever was…

Paul	I block a lot. *(sarcastically)* Well this *(lifting his glass)* helps with that quite a bit. *(to audience)* Cheers! *(pause)* She liked suffering.

Kerry My scars are healing. *(shrugs as if she's not really convinced)* That's what they tell me anyway.

Paul I was always trying to push these feelings away. I really did want to try and make sense out of it.

Kerry I was always blaming myself. There was no remorse from him. At the community centre I went to they'd say, just walk away from him, just leave him. Leave everything, start again.

Paul Like it was that easy.

Kerry *(defensively)* I took my husband back because I loved him. And I always felt that it was maybe my fault. They told me that once the physical abuse starts it never stops. I guess they really know what they're talking about. But at the time you just think, well you just think it will be different for you. You believe that. You want to believe it. You need to believe it.

Paul *(getting agitated)* Things always came up again and again. The same stuff over and over, like a stuck bloody record. That was her, a stuck bloody record going on and on and fuckin' on in my head.

Kerry I'd go back to him but then I'd get so angry, so damn angry about what he had done to me, then the arguments would start, and then the drinking, more arguing and, well you know the rest…I mean, you can imagine can't you? You don't need me spelling it out for you.

Paul	Years down the line she'd start mouthing off about something like it had just happened yesterday. Crazy damn bitch. I tried, I really tried to just block it out but it's so damn hard. *(almost pleading defensively with the audience)* What was I supposed to do? You tell me? What the fuck would you have done in my position? Just one slap I thought, just one Goddamn slap and she'll shut the fuck up. *(standing up, more and more agitated)* But the crazy bitch moaned and complained even more so I had to slap her again. I had to.
Kerry	That was the first time. *(pauses)* He punched me in the face. Then while he was still going at me, he phoned my parents and started shouting down the phone saying…
Paul	*(acting it out as if it is happening in the moment but with an imaginary Kerry in front of him)* I'm gonna kill your daughter listen to this – I'm gonna head butt her. (pause then innocently to audience) Of course I wasn't gonna do it, I just wanted to scare her, scare her enough so she'd shut up.
Kerry	*(raising her hands as if to protect herself, speaking incredulously)* there he was with the phone in his hand speaking to my father the whole time.
Paul	But before I knew it, I'd head butted her and then I couldn't stop. I wanted to, honest I did. I just wanted her to shut up but when I hit her she started crying and screaming and the noise just got to me.

Kerry The assault started, head butting me constantly and my father listening on the other end of the phone – blood everywhere *(turns her head to the side looking out at something beyond her)* and the worst part of it was my son sat on the stairs listening.

Paul I thought if I just hit her enough to shut her up, then I'd stop. When it was happening it was like it wasn't me. You know you're not yourself. I just snap and I don't know that guy, the one who does that. I guess I don't know my own strength.

Kerry I was screaming and crying but that just made him hit me more, then I stopped. I was quiet. I kept thinking that I didn't want my dad to hear me screaming, he's old and I kept thinking this will kill him and it would be my fault. So I just went quiet, really quiet.

Paul She just sat there, on the floor, whimpering like an animal. It made me sick and I had to get out of there. Then when I turned round and saw my boy was standing there in the doorway watching,

Kerry The minute he saw him watching he got even angrier and I got scared he would turn on him, hit him. But he'd never hit the kids, he never did.

Paul You little coward. You're not even big enough to protect your own mother! Just stand there crying like a baby. Well get used to it son, this is real life. This is what married life's all about *(laughs)*

Kerry	And Paul just laughed. I tried to smile at my son, you know to let him know it was okay like but, well you know, I had like blood all over my face and he just kept staring at me with his big eyes and he knew it wasn't alright. He's a smart boy, he knew things even then. He didn't cry though, no my boy didn't cry, just stared real thoughtful like.
Paul	'Is daddy a bad man?' he asked her. And she's sitting there with a messed-up face and blood all over her. It was comical, you know, fuckin' comical.
Kerry	When children come along you shouldn't stay with them you know cos the children, they start suffering – when mum's suffering, they're suffering.
Paul	*(irritated)* She tried to turn the children against me … subtle like
Kerry	*(remembering and getting worked up)* He'd chuck everything in my face, everything I'd do and say and make me feel I was inadequate and stupid.
Paul	*(remembering and getting worked up)* She'd throw it all back at me – that I was a bad husband and a bad father, how people out there didn't know what a loser I really was but she was going to tell them.
Kerry	*(remembering and getting worked up)* He said I wasn't capable of having children, of bringing them up. He said I was an unfit mother.
Paul	She made me feel as though I wasn't anything. Worthless.

Kerry & Paul	*(looking at one another and speaking simultaneously)* …but I still loved him and still wanted to be with him.
	…but I still loved her and still wanted to be with her.
Kerry	Love is blind.
Paul	Love hurts *(laughs)* in more ways than one.
Kerry	He said he loved me. *(pause, thinking and remembering)* In the end it just got nasty and violent and each time I had to be careful what I said and done. Had to tread on eggshells like and be very very careful what I did and said cos he'd take it the wrong way. Had to sort of talk to him on his level and it's difficult when he's drunk because you don't know what he's absorbing. *(pause)* I wouldn't forget – he would. *(getting more and more upset and angry)* You can't let someone else do those things, you can't, you can't. *(calming down)* I wouldn't wish what I got on me for anything and I wouldn't give it to anyone else. *(pause, continues drained and exhausted)* I have no regrets but I want it all to end now. I've had enough.
Paul	*(drained and exhausted)* I have my regrets but I just want it all to end now. I've had enough.
Kerry	No daddy's not a bad man son, I told him. He's just *(pause as she tries to think of something to say)* well he's just confused.
Paul	*(in disbelief)* Confused! I'm confused am I?

Kerry Grown-ups get confused sometimes you know, that's what I told him. *(long pause)* Well, I can't lie, the truth is that within three days of the attack happening I went back. *(to audience, very defensively seeking to justify herself)* I know what you must be thinking but well you see I only went back because I felt sorry for him like. And I couldn't understand how someone I could love so much could turn into this monster and ... and well you know ... truth is I always blamed myself. You know what I mean thinking that it was me, something I did, or should have done, something I could...well, you know, fix.

Paul *(ironically)* All my life people thinking they could fix me. Except the ones that fuckin' broke me. *(sniggering)* Went to counselling, anger management courses – *(ironically)* well the courts made me do *that* one – marriage guidance, alcoholics anonymous...every type of fuckin' counselling and therapy you can imagine. *(thoughtful pause as if trying to understand it all himself)* I don't know. I mean I know I'm angry, I know the drink helps, at first anyways *(pauses)* Christ I know I don't want to be like this *(pause)* I know...I know that I loved her, truth is I still do.

Kerry *(change in tempo)* I like touching and feeling things. I thought, I thought if I stay within four walls not able to go out like and do what I want, well then, he's won hasn't he? Got what he wanted. *(pause)* I feel as though he's in control. Always in control.

Paul   *(pause and seems to drift off into her own world)* I feel like a kite. Only like you know I keep trying to get up there but the winds dropped. Or like a ball you know where all the air has been punctured out. Thing is I couldn't bear to see her hurting. Can you believe it? Couldn't stand to think I had done that to her. In therapy they said the abuser tries to justify his behaviour with excuses. *(in a mocking voice)* 'My parents never loved me', 'My parents beat me', 'I had a bad day at work', 'I lost my temper when I saw that mess' or 'There was nothing else I could do'. *(irritated)* Fuck I wish that were true, I wish it were that fuckin easy. You know, someone just pushes your damn buttons and in your head, you imagine slapping them. We all do it, imagine it like. You know what I mean. But you don't think you ever would, then one day … one day, you don't mean to, you really don't mean to, but you suddenly slap them. *(getting worked up and acting out the movements losing control completely)* You can't believe you've done it but it's just easier to keep slapping, *(gets into a frenzy as he starts remembering)* slapping and kicking and punching and slapping and kicking and... *(difficult pause as he calms down, self-aware of his own lack of control suddenly)* It's just easier than stopping and thinking about what you're doing. You know. You just stop thinking, it doesn't feel real, none of it. *(pause)* God, she knew how to push my buttons, she really does.

Kerry *(furious shouting at Paul)* Push your buttons! Knew how to push your damn buttons did I? If you really had buttons I could push, I'd be pushing 'eject', 'go to hell', not 'hit me'.

Paul *(looking for empathy from the audience and mocking her taking on with his hand)* See what I mean, on and on like a stuck bloody record.

Kerry *(change in tempo)* You know I just wanted him to stop drinking. It was all I wanted. I thought like, well if he stopped the drinking then the fighting would stop and the beatings and we'd get back to the way we used to be like, you know what I mean. So I says to him *(turns to him)* Paul if you give up the drinking, I'll give up something too.

Paul *(to the audience)* Fucking unbelievable? *(incredulously, to Kerry)* Like what? What the hell are you going to give up?

Kerry *(thinks for a while)* I'll give up tea.

Paul *(a mixture of incredulity and fury)* Tea. Fuckin' tea! I'm an alcoholic you stupid cow, you think me giving up the booze is the same as you giving up tea. *(to audience and smashing his fist into his hand)* You know sometimes I just want to smash her stupid face. But I don't you know. I don't! Sometimes, *(speaking very deliberately)* sometimes I hold back. Don't you forget that, that's real control you know. *(pause)* But she doesn't make it easy.

Kerry	*(with a naïve innocence)* Oh but I loves a cuppa I do. *(catching the look on Paul's face)* Okay okay I'll give up something harder, like… *(said as if she has had a wonderful new idea)* oh I know, I know, Friday night bingo.
Paul	*(anger building)* Bingo. Bingo! *(pacing)* Friday night fuckin' bingo!
Kerry	*(oblivious to his rising irritation)* It'll be like Lent, you know, like when I was a kid and I used to give up chocolate. Oh, oh *(excited at a new idea)* there's an idea Paul, I'll give up chocolate, oh that's so much better than the bingo. *(talking oblivious to Paul's presence or his rising temper)* More of a sacrifice like cos you know Paul I have a real sweet tooth. Oh I loves my chocolate I do.
Paul	*(furious to the audience in a collaboratory sense)* And I'm thinking sweet tooth! Sweet fuckin' tooth! She'll have no fuckin teeth by the time I'm finished if she doesn't shut the fuck up. I swear I could have killed her there and then. No jury would have ever sent me away for it either I'm telling you. I would have got off on compassionate grounds, yeh, for being married to a lunatic, a crazy fuckin' lunatic.
Kerry	*(enthusiastic)* So what do you think Paul?
Paul	*(furiously in her face)* What do I think! What do I think? I drink cos I can't live without it. It gets me through the day. I break out in sweats if I don't get my drink. *(through*

	gritted teeth) Is that how you feel about chocolate for Christ's sake?
Kerry	Well not exactly but…
Paul	*(cutting her off and startling her)* Not exactly! Of course not fuckin' exactly. *(suddenly calming down and changing tact, obvious he is scheming)* If you really want to help me, you'd give up something bigger.
Kerry	*(confused and uncertain)* Like what?
Paul	I don't know, like, like *(pretending he's trying to think but clear he has a plan and is scheming)*, well like your diabetes medicine.
Kerry	*(horrified)* but I need that, if I don't take my medicine all sorts could happen to me.
Paul	Yeh just like I need the booze. *(calmly)* You know we'd both be giving up something we need, like we'd be struggling together…
Kerry	…helping one another like.
Paul	Exactly.
Kerry	*(uncertain)* But I don't know the doctor says that…
Paul	Fine. Fine, if it's too much to ask, just don't. I understand. I just thought you loved me. I just thought you wanted to help me get through this.
Kerry	Oh I do Paul, really I do. I'd do anything to help you stop the drinking, anything to help you, us, get back on track.
Paul	Things would be like they used to be.
Kerry	Oh yes, I want that more than anything.

Paul (*smugly*) And the stupid cow stopped taking her medicine, just like that. It was so fuckin easy. Almost too fuckin' easy, I'm telling you. It was like being drunk on hate, that's what I felt when I looked at her.

Kerry (*to audience*) Listen I don't likes to lie to you. And it's not that I lied, I just haven't been whole ways truthful. Well you see, this is how it is, I don't know how to tells you this but *(pause)* well *(pause)* well I stopped taking my medicine. It's complicated like…it was about six months ago, I think. Yes, about six months ago. *(pause)* Can't really remember to tell you the truth. I knows that I need the medicine, honest I knows. I thought I would just start taking it again and everything would be fine, my sight would be back to normal *(starting to cry quietly)* I can see shadows and I thought that meant I could get better…but they tell me it won't. *(head down eyes fixed to the floor)* We made a deal we did. Paul and I, that's my husband, you know. He promised me he'd give up the drinking if I gave up the medicine. I just thought if he stopped drinking then the other stuff would stop too, you know. *(pauses)* He always said I was a stupid cow, I guess I showed him just how right he was. *(raises her head)* I just wanted him to stop the drinking; I'd have done anything to have him stop the drinking. *(sad and distracted, the situation is slowly sinking in)* I'm not crazy you know! And I'm not stupid I'm not. *(laughing slightly,* *long pause then looks directly at audience)* He never did stop the drinking...

(Lights fade then come up on Paul exactly as we last left him and he begins by repeating the line we left him on, Kerry enters)

Paul *(smugly)* And the stupid cow stopped taking her medicine, just like that. It was so fuckin' easy. Almost too fuckin' easy, I'm telling you.

Kerry *(entering)* You broke me Paul.

Paul *(confused and irritated)* What you on about now?

Kerry My sight, they say it's permanent.

Paul What?

Kerry My sight Paul. I'll never get it back.

Paul And that's my fault?

Kerry This is all your fault.

Paul *(getting angry)* Fuck you! I didn't make you stop taking the medicine did I, you stupid cow.

Kerry You knew this would happen. You knew didn't you? You said you'd stop, you promised you'd stop drinking. You promised me Paul.

Paul *(mocking her)* 'You promised me Paul. You said you'd stop Paul.' *(laughing)* Well what you can't see won't hurt you and at least you won't have to watch me drinking now.

Kerry *(getting angry)* I might not be able to see you Paul but I can still smell you.

Paul *(coming up to her face and grabbing her arms, rising fury)* Oh yeh, what do you smell bitch? Tell me! Come on then tell me bitch what you think you smell.

Kerry *(terrified but at the same time feels she has nothing left to lose which gives her a defiance. Pushes him away)* You smell rotten. Evil through and through. Rotten! Rotten!

Paul Shut up Kerry. Shut up! I'm warning you.

Kerry You're rotten. Rotten! It's all your fault Paul. All your fault. You're rotten, rotten to the core. It's your fault. All your fault. *(losing control and slapping at him and pushing him towards the door)*

Paul But…

Kerry Get out! Get out!

Paul But just listen, Kerry please, I…

Kerry *(screaming hysterically)* Get out! Get out! *(Paul leaves, lights fade)* Not long after that he got done again and was sent to prison. I felt safe, secure like, knowing he was locked up and couldn't get at me. But then they let him out early. For good behaviour can you believe that! So he came out in July instead of November and straight away he started chipping away again. I'm going to be honest and truthful with you. I'll never ever be the same. That's the truth. Everywhere I go, everything I do, I'm jumping all the time.

Paul It was just a matter of time. I knew she'd realise how much she needed me. I wanted

	to show her I would take care of her, show her how much I loved her. I know she loves me. Of course she does. She's just playing games. I know her, I know what she wants. She needs me, I know she does and she just needs reminding of that.
Kerry	He broke his restraining order – he came up to the house and he's not allowed anywhere near the house. *(raising her voice)* Not allowed! *(calming down slightly)* I was in hospital. They warned me he was coming out in a few days and they took it seriously – he kept away *(agitated)* but then in November he came into the institute and he was drunk – if he really loved me he wouldn't do that, would he?
Paul	Especially now with her eyes so bad and all, sometimes you know, yeh sometimes I think she did that deliberately. I don't think she planned to go blind…I don't mean that… but she wanted to suffer you know so she could blame it on me, to be able to tell people it was my fault. She wanted to get them all feeling pity for her with that bastard of a husband, and to turn the kids against me, that's what she really wanted. My own family wouldn't even speak to me.
Kerry	*(overly defensive)* It's not my fault they all turned against him. I know he blames me. But it's not my fault, I just told it how it was…you know…then people made their own minds up.

Paul   She took everything and everyone away from me, until she was all I had left. So how could I lose her too?

Kerry   I started going to this centre, there are lots of women like me, well not blind like me but you know, husbands and partners beating them. I loves that group, I have friends there and the counsellors talk to us, I loves them all. Not like a lesbian you know, I loves them like family, that kind of love. They talked to me about the diabetes and why I stopped taking the medicine, I didn't like that so much. He was a different man when I first met him but I didn't realise how much he drank. He used to go on benders and go out and come back weeks and days afterwards. I got to know his sister and she said Paul went out to get a chicken once and never came back. He spent the money on booze. It was always stormy. I never used to stand up to him I would sit down and say nothing. I wouldn't have anything said about him, I would defend him, he was the father of my children. I loved him to bits, every inch, hair, nail, bones, I loved him to bits and he knew that and he knew exactly what to play on, he knew how I felt about him no matter how much he abused me, I still wanted to be with him. *(drifting)* And the sex... *(Suddenly embarrassed)*...it's just that it was so good....especially after....you know.....*(checking herself)* Don't tell anyone I said that bit about the sex. That's private like. He tells me he loves me. He tells me all the time, tells me I need him now more than ever cos I'm blind now. But *(pauses and processes this idea)* that would be awful! *(annoyed)* I just want him to go away – why doesn't he just leave me alone. I want to see him and find out why he's chipping away at me. I mean I want to see him to ask him why he won't leave me alone. He always says he still loves me. It's no good ranting and raving at him. I need, like an electric fence – that's what they do to the cows to separate them – fields and road they stun them. Every time Paul comes near me, he'd get stunned. I think I'd like that. *(pause)* I'll never ever get my life back again. I feel he's on me. I've scrubbed and washed but I'll never get his face off of me.

(Lights dim on Kerry move to general lights as Paul appears)

Kerry   I know you're there Paul. I can feel you. I can smell you

Paul   *(whispering)* Crazy bitch.

Kerry   Why wont you leave me alone?

Paul   You need me Kerry, look at you, anything could happen to you. You need me there looking after you.

Kerry   *(to the audience)* I went walking – I knew he'd be around somewhere, waiting. He knocked me down. He doesn't care I'm blind.

Paul   *(speaking to her though she is unaware of his presence – he comes close enough to be breathing on her face while he speaks in a way that is simultaneously threatening and*

loving) I was trying to show you how vulnerable you are, how much you need me there to protect you.

Kerry *(to the audience)* I think I cope all right with my disabilities. Try and do what I can at home. I'm fine until Paul chips away at me. Unnerves me. Then I don't feel in control. He sprinkled something on me.

Paul *(as he speaks, she is reacting as she did in the moment)* You should have seen her, at first she felt it and brushed it off and then she went crazy.

Kerry Paul! Paul! I can smell you Paul. I know it's you. Oh God what have you put on me. Help me.

Paul Like a bloody dash hound. Should have seen her *(laughing)* sniffing around in the garden screaming that she knew I was there. Neighbours just looking at the poor crazy blind cow next door *(mimicking her)* trying to sniff me out.

Kerry Why are you doing this to me? I know you are there Paul. I know. *(To the audience)* And then I heard him laughing. I told the girls after like and my son and I know they think I'm crazy. Like they don't know what's true anymore cos they say I'm paranoid. They say I'm always smelling him, that I need to get a grip. I want to be in control. But I can't. I'm not myself. Everyone said that to me. I've scrubbed and sprayed I can't get him off my face. I don't

	want my girls in care. They're the world to me. I don't want them to be my carers.
Paul	I'll chip away at you until you end up in Whitchurch. You'll never come out and I will be in the house.
Kerry	*(to the audience)* I get stress in the stomach – didn't know you could get that. I'm not all right in my stomach even when I just hear his name. I'm not happy. Stalked me off a bus. My senses are strong. I could feel him. I went to Poundstretcher and I could smell him when I was queuing up and I hoped and prayed it wouldn't be him but I knew it was. The smell. And I thought do your shopping quick and get out. I was in the queue and I could feel him.
Paul	The police could give her a job as a fuckin sniffer dog.
Kerry	The smell crept over me. Right in my face. Didn't know whether to scream. I got all agitated.
Paul	So she starts speaking to me under her breath
Kerry	Paul I know you're there. Leave me alone or I'll scream.
Paul	And I'm standing in the queue right behind her and I look at the other people and shrug like asking who is this crazy woman and they smile and shrug back and she keeps going on and on.
Kerry	If you touch me I'll scream.

Paul And the girl serving her, she was just a kid and she didn't know whether to giggle or be scared of the crazy blind woman. And Kerry gets more and more nervous and fumbling and drops her purse.

Kerry Oh God. Go away Paul. I can feel you, I can smell you. Leave me alone!

Paul And I bends down like the good fuckin Samaritan and picks up her purse and puts it careful like in her hand leaning in close so she could feel my breath saying 'I think you dropped this'. Fuck you should have seen the look in her face. She started to scream but all that came out was this little yelp. I mean for fucks sake if she wants people to believe there's a crazy stalker after her, fuckin Poundstretchers not the place to go shopping. They all look fuckin crazy in there.

Kerry *(breathless, her fear tangible)* I got served. He followed me. He wanted to know if I needed help and I said I was fine – he didn't keep away from me – he followed me to other shops which I sensed right away and then to the institute where he inquired about me – that means he followed me – I sensed that – that he was following me. It's awful frightening – you don't know if they're going to hurt you – you just don't know.

Paul Hurt her. Hurt her! I only wanted to help her! But would she let me? Oh no, the bitch wouldn't even give me a chance.

135

Kerry My senses are strong. Fear and the smell and the voice. If you took those away, I wouldn't know where else to turn. He's pickled – rotting inside. Alcoholics – they got that smell about them.

Paul I just want her back.

Kerry My confidence is gone. Got to force myself to get back on track. *(thinking)* Did I tell you he got in my face at Poundstretchers? You think it's all in my imagination, I know you do, you, my kids, everyone, but that's just not true. You don't need to say it. I know what you're thinking. I keep thinking he's going to break out. And if the prison is overcrowded like. I don't think he'll get a long sentence. He never does. I feel like his face is on me all the time. If I'm left alone I'll be fine. If Paul leaves me alone I'll be fine. I will be out of sight, out of mind, out of reach out of touch. I can't just move away, you know like disappear. *(indignant)* That won't make it go away. I'm not a bird I can't fly away. I don't want to stay at home I want to go shopping with the girls – I want to be going out and focussing. He won't listen, the drink has addled his brain. It's just I go to pieces sometimes. I cry most of the time. I don't want my girls thinking all men are nasty cos they're not. They're not. *(pause)* I feel as though I'm not a mother, I've let them down big time. Something has got to be done. I hope to God I don't have to go to court. Some of the things they've said – they make him sound great. I've got no

	regrets about having his children but I need to leave it now. I'm not strong now.
Paul	*(in background)* I love you. I really do love you - every inch, every bone, every nail every hair... I'll always be with you.
Kerry	I only got that smell – it will always be with me – and when someone's an alcoholic it will never go away – makes me feel shaky and sick and it's quite frightening. I loved him you know – I really loved him – every inch, every bone, every nail every hair... He said to me once he'd always be with me. Sometimes I think, when he gets out, I'll find out where he is living, there are ways of getting that information you know. I'll get his address and I'll go there and I'll kill him. I'll press my hands around his throat and I'll kill him. I'll do time for it. I'll go to prison and I'll come out and when I step out of those doors, I'll know Paul is not around to hurt me verbally and physically. And when that happens it will be a big weight gone – whoosh – I wish I'd come to my senses a long time ago. These are things I can't tell anyone. Paul's chipping away at me and I'm afraid. I want my children to remember me as happy. My eyes are gone but I'm still Kerry underneath. *(pause)* You know when anyone says to me, we've seen your ex a feeling comes over me, a fear. I feel physically sick. Only difference is I can't see him coming and they can. *(sounding more desperate)* I can't see him coming. Don't you understand that? I can't see him coming! *(lights dim)*

A time from the past in Kerry and Paul's relationship. Paul enters the room singing and dancing, has clearly been drinking and is in high spirits but still has control of himself.

Kerry   I sent you to the shops five hours ago!

Paul   Take it easy.

Kerry   Five hours Paul!

Paul   Well I'm here now.

Kerry   Am I supposed to be grateful? I guess I should be, at least you came back the same day. *(Paul laughs)* I ask you to go get some bread and…

Paul   …and? *(continues humming and dancing)*

Kerry   And I should know better, shouldn't I! Bloody typical I should have known you'd end up down the pub. Well your dinner's ruined. It's in the bin if you want it.

Paul   I'm not hungry. *(playfully)* Come dance with me.

Kerry   I don't want to dance with you. You're drunk *(pause)* again!

Paul   *(laughing)* Again!

Kerry   It's not funny! I'm sick of this Paul, it's the same every time. I keep hoping things will get better but they never do… you're not listening, the drink has addled your brain.

He pulls her towards him and continues dancing, she resists at first but is caught up in his good mood and for a time they dance and hum together, they begin speaking but the dancing continues.

Paul You know I love you?

Kerry *(trying to show him she is annoyed but coming round and being almost flirtatious with him)* Well you've got a funny way of showing it.

Paul Come on we haven't danced in a while, you used to love it babes.

Kerry There are a lot of things I used to love Paul. *(Paul trying to suppress his irritation)*

Paul Oh come on, for one night, let's just dance and be happy

Kerry *(attempt at sarcasm)* Like we used to be?

Paul *(ignoring or oblivious to the sarcasm)* Yeh babes like we used to be. Like we still could be.

Kerry The way we used to laugh, the way we used to love one another.

Paul *(flirtatiously)* Don't you still love me?

Kerry Yes I do *(pause)* but sometimes I wish I didn't.

Paul So you love me? Every inch *(smiles at her in expectation that she will continue, clearly something they are used to saying to one another)* Come on Kerry say it, every inch...

Kerry Every bone,

Paul Every nail,

Kerry Every hair...

Paul	I'll always be with you Kerry, always.
Kerry	*(softening)* You promise?
Paul	I promise *(they kiss)*
Kerry	I just wish…
Paul	*(still passionate)* mmh? What babes, tell me, I'm here to make all your wishes come true.
Kerry	Well that you'd stop the drinking and then all the other stuff wouldn't happen, the arguments, the fighting, the…
Paul	*(irritated, his mood changing in an instant)* Just one night Kerry. Just one fuckin night can't you just let it go? Just forget for one fuckin night?
Kerry	*(incredulous)* Forget? Forget! What do you want me to forget? That we have no money again? Forget that you sold our children's toys and I had to say they left them at nanny's? Forget the times you hit me?
Paul	Why have you always got to ruin everything? Always the same with you. Always the fuckin same.
Kerry	*(realising she has set him off and desperate to cool the situation)* Just forget it, I didn't mean…
Paul	Oh now you'd like to forget. A bit fuckin late for that.
Kerry	Come on Paul let's keep on dancing, you're right, let's not spoil it.

She hums as they begin dancing again slowly, she caresses him and they start to kiss.

Paul *(suddenly pushing Kerry away his anger rising)* No! No! you can't play these games with me.

Kerry trying to embrace him, calm him and kiss him, desperate to placate him aware of where his anger might lead. Paul struggles, gives in, struggles again until his anger takes over and he pushes her away forcefully.

Paul You're not fit to be a woman you know, not fit to be a mother. Call yourself my wife, tell me you love me, but it's a lie, all of it.

Kerry But I do love you, I just can't take all of this no more.

Paul And you think I can? Coming home to you every night, listening to your moaning and complaining. All you have to do is look after me and the kids and you can't even do that you lazy bitch. Look at the place *(kicks some things over)* the house is a fuckin mess Kerry, a fuckin mess. And so are you. *(grabs her by her hair at the back of her head and pulls her towards him, stares at her furiously for a while then suddenly changes and kisses her and tries to continue dancing with her)* Tell me you love me Kerry, tell me.

Kerry *(trying not to cry as she says the lines he wants to hear haltingly)* Every inch. Every bone. Every nail,

Paul Every hair…

Kerry That's the way it was. The same story every time. What choice did I have? I had to take it. What else could I have done? Once I stood up to him. You know I even surprised myself. I said to him – 'I don't want you keeping me short of money. Pull yourself together.' I'd shame him sometimes. But when I realised he was drinking again I knew there was no hope. He wasn't going to change. He wasn't going to budge a centimetre. He needed the booze. There's always been booze in our relationship – myself, Paul and a bottle or a can. It got in between us and it wedged and wedged. I used to cry to release all the worry and the stress so I could focus the next day but it didn't do anything, it just, it just wouldn't go away. I knew in the end I just felt as if I'd gone down the wrong path. I always had him back over the years, continually wanted to be with him, everything would be hunky dory for an hour, two hours, a day maybe ... in the end it got less and less, minutes, seconds and I thought, no you can't do this anymore ... continually drinking round the clock – enough is enough you can't help him anymore I told myself, the drink has taken over like fungus all over him. You know sometimes if he'd sit next to me, that was very rare, he used to shake and he would say he was cold, but he wasn't cold it was the booze. Some people think I wanted to go blind. How can anyone say such a thing? *(unintentionally showing her manipulative side)* That's the sort of thing he'd say you know. You're *all* the same, nobody understands. *(pause)* I feel as though I've failed, failed myself, failed Paul, failed my children. I don't feel as though I'm a mum anymore. Eventually I'll lose it and then they'll see the true state of me. I'll go into a place like Whitchurch and that's where I'll stay. I don't want to crumble. I'm ashamed and embarrassed. I cry to release everything I'm feeling and then once I cry I'm fine. I've got to cry then I'm fine it's too much inside my head and my stomach. *(long pauses)* I do like going into churches – I like touching the cross and our lord – I don't know if that makes me feel stronger. I go there once a week, any church you don't need to be a member you know, if you can't touch the statue you just sit in a chair and you get that feeling around you and then that gives you strength and you can get through the day. I'm not a statistic. I don't want to hear that stuff. I'm not like those other women. Things with Paul and me, well it was different, we loved one another. *(thinking)* He always said next time he wouldn't hit me, he'd control it. *(pause)* He lied every time. Sometimes I'd fight back. I think I was fighting back, maybe I was just fighting, maybe I started it sometimes you know. We'd pull each other's hair, scratch, fight. He'd spit on me sometimes. And I'd wait till he turned his back on me, till he was walking away and I'd spit on his back. He wouldn't know and he'd go out with that spit on him, that'd make me smile. *(pause)* You know when I was thinking of leaving – he always knew – funny how they can feel it off you.

The helplessness. There aren't any answers. I can't go on like this. No one can make it go away. I'm blind now. Why doesn't he just leave me alone? It's over.

Paul *(a voice in the background)* I love you Kerry. Every inch...Every bone...Every nail...Every hair... I'll always be with you Kerry, always. I promise.

Kerry I don't care! I don't care who knows anymore. I'm not ashamed. When I started coming here, to this group, I learned not to be ashamed, not to blame myself. It feels good to talk about it sometimes. *(pause)* You know I wake up at one in the morning, most nights I hardly sleep at all – I can't. The more I lie there awake the more I'm thinking, all the time just thinking. I want to stop but I can't turn off all those thoughts. And he's always on my mind. So I shut myself in. *(pause)* I used to sit in the dark with the window open. I don't know why. *(pause)* You know I can see him. Even when he can't see me. *(pause)* In the dark I mean, when I'm alone, I see him. I see him everywhere. *(laughs dismissively)* I've been afraid of his reactions for over twenty years. Every time I thought he couldn't get me anymore he always did. Comes a time when you just get too tired to care, weary of it all. What's he going to do that he hasn't already? At night you know, I go to my room. I close the curtain, put the light on – how crazy's that? Turning the light on when you can't even see! Automatic like, you know, you just do it, without thinking. I sit on the end of my bed for hours. I don't realise it I just start thinking and the time passes by. Just sitting there thinking. *(fade out)*

We go to Kerry and Paul meeting for the first time. They are in a bar with their own groups of friends (not necessary for anyone else to be present) and clearly have caught one another's eye. Paul constantly looking over, Kerry embarrassed but still flirting. Eventually Paul makes his way towards her.

Paul I was sitting in the pub with the lads and I looked up and saw her. In that moment I just knew she was the one. *(cocky and charming)* Do you believe in love at first sight...or do I have to walk by again? *(Kerry giggles, Paul feels confident from the reaction and encouraged to continue)* Was your father a thief? 'Cause someone stole the stars from the sky and put them in your eyes!

Kerry *(pretending to be unimpressed but clearly attracted to him)* Is that the best you can come up with? Those are the worst chat up lines I've heard all night.

Paul *(laughing)* Oh I've got worse than that, I'm just getting warmed up.

Kerry *(giggling)* God help us.

Paul Listen babes, I may not be the best looking guy here, but I'm the only one talking to you.

Kerry *(feigning annoyance)* Bloody cheek! *(they both laugh, every so often there are pauses in the conversation when they just look at*

	each other, the chemistry between them is clear)
Paul	I know but *(becoming very serious)* at least *I'm* not a thief!
Kerry	*(confused and slightly affronted)* What are you talking about? I'm no thief!
Paul	But you're the one who stole my heart.
Kerry	Oh please stop. You're just embarrassing yourself now.
Paul	Worth it if I get to talk to an angel like you. The name's Paul by the way and the only thing your eyes haven't told me is your name *(reaches out his hand)*
Kerry	*(embarrassed)* Kerry. *(he takes her hand and kisses it)*
Paul	So Kerry, shall we chat or continue flirting from a distance?
Kerry	You're pretty sure of yourself!
Paul	Kerry my love I'm a nervous wreck I tell you. You see the problem is I've forgotten my phone number so I was wondering if I could have yours?
Kerry	You're unbelievable.
Paul	That's what the ladies tell me.
Kerry	Are you drunk?
Paul	No Kerry my love I'm just intoxicated by you! You know you kind of look like someone I know…who is it again…ah yeh my next girlfriend.
Kerry	You think?

Paul	Ah Kerry darling I'm happy to just stand here and stare at you, that way I'll remember your face for my dreams.

Kerry	And that's the way it was. He could charm anyone.

Paul	She was the most beautiful thing I'd ever seen. I knew that night that this was the woman I wanted to be my wife

Kerry	There really was something irresistible about him. And how he made me laugh with his terrible chat up lines, so cocky and false yet so sincere. I think I fell in love with him right there and then. *(pause)* I can't stand the thought of him being with someone else…ever. I love him.

Paul	Every inch…Every bone…Every nail…Every hair… I'll always be with you, always. I promise.

Kerry	Have you ever loved somebody so much you felt like you couldn't breathe?

Paul	I couldn't get enough of her, now I'm sick of seeing her fuckin face.

(Lights dim as we move to a time closer to the present.)

Paul	Where did we go wrong?

Kerry	Where? Where Paul? How can you even ask that? Everything you did was to destroy me. It didn't matter about the children. It was all about destroying me.

Paul	*(genuinely sorry)* I never meant to hurt you.

Kerry	*(indignant)* You wouldn't pay for the children's support and I stupidly, so damn

	stupidly….well….things were so bad, and well, I just kept taking you back. I felt that the children needed this family unit and I just thought you had changed, I wanted to believe you had changed – but you never ever change. Never.
Paul	Don't say that Kerry. Don't say that. We can still make this work.
Kerry	I can't do it any more Paul. I just can't.
Paul	*(trying to control his temper)* Don't say that Kerry, I'm telling you I will change this time. Things will get better.
Kerry	No Paul. They won't. They never do.
Paul	You need me.
Kerry	For what?
Paul	You need me Kerry!
Kerry	For what I'm asking you? Tell me for what?
Paul	I need you.
Kerry	You need me? You *need* me! What for? A punching bag.
Paul	*(moves closer to her and takes her head in his hands pulling her forward, a little too forcefully, until their foreheads are against one another's and speaks through gritted teeth)* You need me Kerry. I need you. We need one another, that's how this works.
Kerry	*(trying to be forceful but starting to get afraid)* Not anymore Paul.
Paul	*(pulls her closer and kisses her forcefully and prolonged, releases her from the kiss*

	but keeps a hold of her face) See Kerry you love me. I can taste it on you.
Kerry	*(pushing him away and standing up, she has reached breaking point and shouts at him through tears)* That's not love you taste, it's fear. Fear you bastard. You don't even know what love is. I don't think you ever did. *(slumps to the ground)*
Paul	*(running to her and takes her in his arms)* Don't say that Kerry you know I've always loved you. I never meant to hurt you, never. *(getting agitated)* And if you ever try to fuckin leave again…
Kerry	What? You're just as blind as me you know.
Paul	And your temper's just as bad as mine.

Kerry tries to push him away. He stands up agitated, pacing back and forth muttering about loving her, not wanting to lose her.

| **Kerry** | Just get out Paul. Leave me alone. For once please just go and stay gone. |

He stares down at her shocked by her words. Slowly he moves towards her as if to take her in his arms but as he crouches down his agitation increases and he grabs her by the hair pulling her head back and starts to shout in her face.

| **Paul** | Why Kerry? Why do you always have to push? Why do you make do this, make me hit you? I don't want to and you just keep making me do it, over and over again. You and me, we're the same Kerry. The fuckin same. We're joined at the hip and no one and nothing can ever separate us. *(kisses her but* |

	one hand is still pulling her head back by the hair, she squirms a little but accepts the kiss while at the same time not returning it)
Paul	Everyone asking questions. What the fuck? This is private, it's no one else's business what goes on behind closed doors between a husband and a wife! And you can't trust that neurotic bitch! *(defensively, trying to hide his anger)* What's she been telling you about me then? So she can say whatever she likes and you just believe it – I'm like this evil bastard and she's little Miss innocent? Like hell. That crazy bitch telling the whole world about me, telling people that I've hurt her, spreading her fuckin lies… *(furious)* … saying that shit about me! She hates me and *(laughs)* and…And I fuckin love it! *(calming down)* I never meant to hurt her, honest, she just, well she just pushed and pushes. *(pauses, angry again)* That bitch, she's trying to destroy me. How can she do this to me. Making a fuckin soap opera out of our lives and me as some rotten evil bastard. You've got no right to judge me. No right at all. It's all fucking judgement. You see some poor blind bitch sitting there crying her fuckin little blind eyes out, telling the whole world what a bastard her husband is. Who will want to hear my side, who will believe it was her fault – that she provoked, that she pushed? She told the police all this stuff I did to her you know, got a restraining order against me. And those sessions with all them other women, all of them talking

Kerry shit… It's too late now. That fuckin bitch has ruined my life.

I don't feel anything anymore. I don't blame myself, not one bit. He got his way after all, I mean he got the last word didn't he *(laughs)*. They were all there at the funeral, crying their eyes out like this great guy had died, like they'd all loved him. Guilty conscience if you ask me. Good riddance to him, to all of them, if you ask me. I wanted to make sure he was dead that's why I went to the funeral. Why should I feel remorse? The only remorse I feel is that I'm blind and can't see with my own eyes that that miserable lying drunk is really dead, that I didn't get to see the miserable coward hang himself. I needed to be sure he was dead. Sure that he wasn't going to be coming back, that he couldn't get me anymore. They took me right up to the coffin so I could touch him. He didn't smell the same anymore. Still I knew it was him. I don't need him. I don't need his help. I don't need anything from him. He's gone completely. Whoosh gone. He's gone completely this time. I don't love him. I only went to the funeral to make sure you know, make sure he was dead – to stick a pin in him to make sure he was dead. I still smell him you know. Everywhere I go, I can still smell him on me and I know he's there, waiting, just waiting.

Paul *(voice off stage/or close behind her but unacknowledged)* I love you Kerry. Every inch…Every bone…

Kerry Every nail…Every hair…

Paul I'll *always* be with you Kerry, *always*. I promise. I love you too much to walk away.

The End

Workshop Ideas

Below are discussion points and exercises that can help not only lead us to a better understanding of the play, but also of Applied Theatre and what it involves. In all Applied Theatre and Theatre of the Oppressed exercises, discussion is key. Always allow ample time for discussion after each exercise and explore what has happened.

Discussion questions

1. Discuss the stage elements of the play and what makes it Applied Theatre e.g. set, lights, props etc.
2. The concept of applied plays is not to take sides but simply to tell the story. How do our feelings about both Kerry and Paul change throughout and why?
3. Applied Theatre often plays with the idea of victim and perpetrator roles being interchangeable. Discuss how this happens in the play.
4. At times both characters can be difficult to like and/or empathise with. Discuss.
5. Discuss your views on whether or not you think Kerry and Paul love one another.
6. Why do you think Paul committed suicide? What was his goal in doing that?
7. Kerry deliberately stopped taking her medicine, even though Paul did not keep his end of the bargain and was open about this. Why did Kerry do this, endangering her health and losing her vision as a result?
8. 'Paul is charming and witty and very likeable at times, more so than Kerry.' Discuss.
9. What evidence is there that Kerry's role as a 'victim' continues after Paul's death albeit in her own head? Why do you think this is?

10. What is the purpose of this play?
11. The set, as is often the case in Applied Theatre, is minimal. The idea is that the audience fill it in with their own imagination. Discuss the imagined scenery you create watching the play.
12. The minimal nature of Applied Theatre often means that the audience see things that are not there and do not happen in the play. Frequently audiences have insisted that they saw the son on the stairs and insisted he was physically in the play. Discuss.
13. Discuss why you think Kerry wanted and allowed her story to be told.
14. What feelings does the writer want to evoke in the audience and why?
15. The actors often look directly at audience members and ask a question. What is the purpose of this and how do you imagine the audience react?
16. Moments of humour are key to many applied scripts in order to give the audience a moment of release. Look at the humorous moments in the play and what preceded them. Why was it so important to include humour at those precise moments?
17. When the audience laughs in applied theatre, they become complicit. What do you think is meant by this?
18. It is normal for an Applied Theatre performance to have a discussion time with the audience after the play. Why do you think this is necessary, especially with the subject matter of this play?
19. It has been said that Applied Theatre plays with our emotion and our certainties. Discuss.
20. 'No situation is black and white; life would be easier if it was.' Discuss how this applies to the play.

Applied Theatre Exercises

When doing these exercises it is important to remember that the different stages will often be carried out on different days and do not need to be done in succession. The exercises can be adapted and used for any of the plays.

Please note that in Applied Theatre time should *always* be allocated to discuss and process the exercises after they have been completed.

Word combat

Two actors sit facing each other in the characters of Kerry and Paul. A word of warning: with the process below it is easy to stop the exercises too early. You may feel that they have run out of ideas and it is time to move on. However in applied theatre exercises that point when the actors are struggling for ideas, is the exact point to continue the exercise as they will be forced to dig deeper. When the words flow easily they are still at the superficial level.

1. Taking it in turns they each say a negative word regarding the other. When one has finished, the other says their word. This continues for a few minutes. Words cannot be repeated by the individual (that is, both Kerry and Paul may use the same word but as an individual they must think of a new word each time).
2. As above only this time taking it in turns, they each say a positive word regarding the other.
3. As above only this time taking it in turns, they each say words regarding their marriage.
4. As above only this time taking it in turns, they each say words regarding their children.
5. Discuss.

Completing a memory

The actors, in the characters of Kerry and Paul, sit facing one another. They are asked to think of a positive memory from their lives together. They cannot discuss this. One begins telling the story of the memory filling in as much detail as possible. After one minute they stop and the other continues for the next minute and so on. They must accept the information the other provides and build on where the other has left off each time. The exercise can be repeated with new memories. Positive memories are a way for the characters to remember why they are together and the love they feel/have felt for one another.

In rehearsal work we often use this exercise to punctuate the rehearsal period in between other exercises. The exercise should continue for a minimum of ten minutes. As the actors become accustomed to these exercises, they should be able to sustain this for significantly longer periods.

Repeat the exercise using negative memories. This enables the characters to explore their emotions and the more destructive side of their relationship. It will also enable them to see how quickly the negativity can escalate between them and how they may try to scale it down.

Discuss the information that has been gathered through the exercise. The memories developed also help build the characters for future work.

The Bigger Story

Whole group forms a large circle and everyone takes on a role. Based on the size of the group roles are allocated in the following order until everyone has a role:

- The characters in the play (Kerry and Paul)
- The characters who are mentioned in the play (the children, Kerry's father, the psychologist, a woman from the support group and so on)
- The characters who must exist based on what we know from the play (Kerry's mother, Paul's parents, possible siblings for Kerry and Paul, the police, judge, prison cellmate and so on)

The amount of people involved is equal to how many are in the group you are working with. Choosing which characters to use for the size of the group should be by agreement of all involved. However the 'characters who must exist' cannot be chosen until the other roles have been filled. Therefore with smaller groups you may only have Kerry, Paul and a couple of those mentioned in the play.

When everyone has been allocated a role, two are chosen to go into the middle of the circle and strike up a conversation in character. After a few minutes, one is removed and a new person enters. This means characters who would not normally cross paths suddenly find themselves in the centre, forced to conduct a conversation with an unlikely counterpart. Each time a new conversation begins the circle must respect any information revealed at each point and can build on it if relevant.

There are no changes to who is in the centre unless called by the facilitator. There can be no physical contact at any time and the two characters in the centre must remain there for the allocated time even if they choose not to speak. The facilitator decides how long any two characters spend in the centre together based on the progression of the exercise, therefore times will vary throughout. At times the story will take a new direction, a new main character might develop, or a new issue, underlying the one originally being dealt with.

As the group becomes more experienced, settings other than the circle can be chosen and characters are moved in and out of the various settings to hold the conversations. For example we may choose settings for this play such as the house, the shops, the women's support group, the pub, or the prison. Reactions and conversations that develop are then influenced also by the locations (this variation does require more intense work and it is wiser to move into it only when participants are comfortable with the concept).

For example, doing this exercise with groups we have often found the developing story is about the son and problems he has at school and with friendships. Another story that developed was that Kerry's mother was a victim of domestic abuse. Many storylines develop and it becomes a story within a story. We have also carried out this exercise as an impromptu performance for public viewings. Nobody knows how the story will develop until it begins and the facilitator must be alert at all times to guide the story appropriately with the choices s/he makes.

Memory Game

Place a chair centre stage. One actor portraying either Kerry or Paul begins telling a memory that they were both involved in. If the other thinks the storyteller has omitted any detail, they stop him/her, change places and continue with their own version until another makes a similar challenge and so on. They can interrupt as often as they believe is justified.

Discuss point of view and differing perspectives revealed by the exercise.

Variations

- begin with the end of the story following the same procedure
- involve more characters if they play a part in the memory (for example, Kerry could be telling the story of the first time Paul hit her which is in the play. Paul can interrupt, but so also could Kerry's father and the son – each presenting their point of view on the events that unfolded).

The Counselling Session

Two chairs are placed centre stage. Paul takes one chair and another actor assumes the role of a counsellor and sits in the other. They begin a counselling session. The other actors watch and when they feel the 'counsellor' is struggling they tap him/her on the shoulder and replace them, picking up the conversation where it was left off. Each counsellor should be given a chance to develop the conversation and overcome the challenges before being tapped out. As the session continues counsellors can return as many times as they choose. The goal is to see if they can achieve a breakthrough. However the actor playing Paul must stay true to his character throughout and use the information in the play to influence his behaviour and responses to the counsellor.

When the counsellors either have a breakthrough or have exhausted all possibilities, repeat the exercise for Kerry.

Discuss as a whole group afterwards. In all discussions ensure that no 'magic' solutions were found and that Paul and Kerry stayed true to what we know of them. It is the role of the facilitator to ensure that the actors stay true to their characters and no 'magic' solutions are introduced.

Escalation taps

Two actors sit side by side in the roles of Kerry and Paul. The facilitator stands behind them. They are asked to begin a day-to-day conversation such as:

- how the children are getting on at school
- something topical from the news
- finances
- a shopping list
- what's for dinner…

Once the conversation has got underway, the facilitator taps them at different times. One tap signifies they have to calm down, two taps that their temper is escalating. The facilitator can play with forcing Paul to calm down and empowering Kerry, as well as other variations with the taps. However the exercise wants us to look at how all behaviour has consequences. Kerry, for example, may become empowered but in the process often becomes the aggressor.

While actors can get out of their chair and invade the space of the other, they should be strictly advised to have no physical contact. The facilitator follows them if they move and can control this aspect at all times through the use of the single tap to calm them.

Discuss afterwards and look at the power struggles that emerge and the consequences for all involved in the short and long term.

Changing my mind

Two actors sit side by side in the roles of Kerry and Paul. The facilitator stands behind them. They are asked to begin a day-to-day conversation such as:

- going on holiday
- something topical from the news
- future plans
- political/religious views

Once the conversation has got underway, the facilitator taps them at different times. This single tap on the shoulder means they have to change their point of view.

For example, if Kerry and Paul were discussing going on holiday and Kerry said she didn't want to go abroad and the facilitator tapped her, she would change her mind to state that she did want to travel abroad. The exercise continues going backwards and forwards, the characters contradicting themselves but having to find natural, clever ways to do so.

The exercise has two main functions. First it looks at how we contradict what we say and think frequently, how we often say things to please others. Second it explores how little we know our own minds.

This exercise is an excellent closing one as it quickly becomes humorous and difficult for the actors to keep up with. It lightens the atmosphere and is a relaxing way to end a workshop or rehearsal. However it is worth noting that it is also embracing the complicit aspect and purpose of laughter in applied theatre. The exercise is welcome light relief and brings laughter, but we are laughing at a serious topic and we are reminded of this over and over. All this should be discussed with the group before closing.

Do it differently!

The facilitator chooses key moments in the play. Two actors in character begin performing (script in hand if necessary) one of the moments. The facilitator claps and the characters must continue the scene but by making a single but significant change. While no longer following the script, the actors must stay true to the nature of the characters. The facilitator must watch and listen closely and if they feel they are not being honest to the characters they pause and discuss this with the actors.

For example let's take the scene when Paul and Kerry first met at the bar. The actors begin to perform it and the facilitator signals a change – this might be that Kerry walks away and does not engage in conversation with Paul. However as the new scene continues Paul might buy a drink for Kerry and take it to where she is sitting. He continues to joke with her. We know from the play that she liked this and found it funny and charming. The change shows us that at that time, even with a change, the characters would probably still have gone down the same path.

Another example might be the scene where Kerry and Paul make a pact that he will stop drinking and she will stop taking her medicine. If we try to make a change there Kerry might refuse to stop taking her medicine. However in the new scene Paul would probably be able to guilt her into it in the end by being manipulative. Equally if the change were that Paul refused to stop drinking, Kerry might still give up her medicine to try to guilt him into stopping drinking.

Each exploration may end in the same result; however it helps us explore the characters, how their minds work and the inevitability about so many aspects of their relationship. All of this should be discussed after each change.

Sold

Introduction

While working on 'til Death do us Part we came across a number of human trafficking cases. In these cases the survivors had sought help for domestic abuse and it had subsequently been learnt that they were also victims of trafficking. This led to the creation of a new project working with people who had been trafficked and learning about a world previously invisible to me. It was by far one of the most disturbing projects I have ever taken part in. To realize that human trafficking was not something happening somewhere else, far from me but rather that it was on my own doorstep in so many forms and that unwittingly or not, in many ways I was complicit.

Deciding which stories to use in the play and how to combine them seemed an overwhelming task until a series of stories were shared that mentioned a bus stop. That for me was the key I needed to unlock the story. In this piece I wanted people to see the various forms of human trafficking that existed, that it occurred within our community, our town or village, as well as to those people brought in from abroad. Each story was heart-breaking and the sense of solace ad desolation present throughout.

Sold was written after a lengthy period of consultation and counselling of a number of trafficked victims. It tells the story of 6 individuals who have all suffered at the hands of traffickers, all coming from different countries, backgrounds and circumstances, all different ages and trafficked in different ways. Their stories collide at a city centre bus stop on a series of winter evenings. Moving and harrowing all stories are based on true accounts of trafficked victims and bring home the fact that these atrocities are happening under our noses. The script is based on the stories that were shared and are true testimonies.

The play provoked a strong reaction. People were shocked by the idea that local people could also be victims of trafficking; by the idea that the person standing next to you at the bus stop could be suffering in this way, by how blind we are to what's going on in our surroundings – the example of the boy in particular affected many, after all how often have we seen a child get into a car at a bus stop and assumed the man picking him up was his father, grandfather, or uncle? As the boy himself says 'Don't worry, no one will ask any questions – they never do.' Many were disturbed by Maria's story and the concept of trafficking happening in a domestic relationship.

Many people wanted answers – demanded to know how this can be stopped? What happened to the individuals in the stories? Why can't we provide a satisfactory conclusion, the stereotypical 'happy ending'? My response is always 'because this is not a fairy-tale', these stories are real, ongoing and as inconclusive as is much in life. Why would I provide a false happy ending? So we can all feel better about ourselves and continue to pretend this doesn't happen? This is what I mean about applied theatre plays having a purpose. In this case our purpose was to raise awareness to a wider public about the issue of human trafficking happening in our own area. Subsequently the Welsh Government commissioned TVO to perform the play to key public service workers who deal with people who have been trafficked.

Characters

Man: In his 30s of ethnic background. A street-smart drug dealer.

Odette: Young woman of Arabic origin, scared and innocent looking, heavily pregnant.

Lisa: Young woman, very slight and blonde, limited English, often speaks in a foreign language of unidentified origin but from somewhere in Eastern Europe.

Anna: A sex worker in her mid 30s, tired and worn looking, cynical and worldly, her occupation is clear from her dress.

Maria: Average looking, blends in and looks like any ordinary person returning home from work, dressed conservatively

Boy: Aged between 10 and 13 years old. Precocious, yet with an air of innocence and vulnerability. Dressed in expensive sports brand clothing and wearing a hoody. Tough, street attitude but all is a front, really is a vulnerable child who has been forced to become streetwise.

Setting - The play is set at a bus stop. There is a bus shelter with a bench inside. The bus shelter has a back and roof cover but is not enclosed to ensure that the actors can be seen moving around it. There is a post with the number of the buses and a timetable. There is frequent reference to cars and buses stopping. These are never seen but are treated as if present. The action takes place over a series of days. On stage right there is a black box where Odette sits.

Lighting - The bus shelter is lit. Behind the bus shelter is dimly lit to give the impression of shadows. There is a spot stage right where Odette sits. When the monologues take place the other characters freeze, unless stage instructions state otherwise.

Lights up. The man and Anna are standing at the bus stop. The boy walks on stage and hovers near the bus stop, constantly shuffling his feet and looking down. Suddenly Anna and the man step forward to signal for a bus to stop and walk towards it leading them off stage. Maria comes running on but is too late to catch the bus. She is clearly frustrated and upset. She sits down and notices the boy, he looks back at her. They stare at one another for a time.

Boy What the fuck you looking at lady?

Maria I… *(Shocked by the boy's rudeness, opens her mouth to speak but then checks herself and says nothing, shakes her head in rebuke, tutting.)*

Boy I said, what the fuck …

Maria *(annoyed, cutting him off)* I heard you the first time you cheeky little shit. What you doing out here on your own at this time of night? Where are your parents?

Boy *(uncomfortable but trying to act tough)* Mind your own business, you nosy bitch.

Maria Well, all I'm saying is a kid your age shouldn't be out alone at night…

Boy *(defensively cutting her off)* I aint no kid lady *(they look at one another)* and I aint alone, my dad's right over there. *(points)* See! *(pretends to wave to someone and runs towards stage left but stays in the shadows)*

Maria *(as if talking to herself)* I'm sure that kids up to no good. I mean he can't be more than ten or eleven and he's always hanging around this bus stop late at night.

	(distracted she looks at the bus timetable) Thirty minutes til the next one. Damn, I'm sure the driver saw me running to catch the bus and drove off deliberately. *(shouting after the bus which is already long gone)* Bastard! *(pause)* I'm going to get it now when I get home. *(agitated)* Try telling *him* it wasn't my fault! He'll say I should have run faster, that it's my fault because I'm slow. Then it all starts – the insults, the …. *(lights fade on her and come up on the boy)*
Boy	*(matter of fact, no emotion shown)* Stand close to the bus stop. *(beat)* That way it looks like you are with someone waiting for the bus. *(beat)* Don't go inside the shelter or the cars won't stop. *(beat)* Stand to the left and when the car pulls up you pretend he's your dad … or your uncle … or your grandpa *(beat)* and you get in the car. *(beat)* That way if the police come it don't look suspicious like. *(beat)* They drop you off back at the bus stop. *(beat)* You don't go back home til you've made 300 quid *(beat)* more on the weekend. *(pause)* Home!
Maria	*(looking at the boy)* He's still there. I'm telling you something's not right. You can tell just looking at him. *(shrugs)* Well what can I do? We've all got our problems, I mean I can't be interfering...imagine if I did it would just bring me more problems and I can't be doing with that. *(beat)* I'm sure that kids on drugs or something, looks the type, kids nowadays they just have no

	respect *(beat)* and he's got one hell of a mouth on him.
Boy	Sometimes it takes a couple of days to get the money. I's gotta stay out on the street all night. *(beat)* Sometimes they give me pills. *(beat)* They say it helps me sleep. *(beat)* They help me forget *(laughs with a sense of experience older than his years)* but I don't remember what I'm supposed to be forgetting…my mum…my dad *(beat)*. I'm better off without them. *They* treat me better than my own parents did!
Maria	Up to no good I'm telling you. Young people nowadays you just can't trust them, not one bit. You know sometimes I think it's a blessing I've got no kids *(holding back tears)* sometimes…
Boy	Sometimes you imagine what you want and when you take the pills you think you've got it like. You see it. You don't know what's real no more but it don't matter. *(beat)* Then you don't care what they do to you.
Maria	Every day it's the same people. You look at them but you don't really see them. Empty faces. Sometimes I think, I wonder what their stories are. I wonder what they think when they look at me. Do they know? *(looking at the boy again, guilty at not helping him)* I mean it's not like anyone ever helped *me. (suddenly stands up as she sees a bus approaching, steps forward and signals for it to stop and exits stage left.)*

Boy (*The boy steps out of the shadow as a car pulls into the bus stop. He steps towards it.*) You want to be my daddy tonight mister. *(beat)* I'm a good boy. *(waits a little as if listening to what the driver is saying)* Yes yes good price *(beat)* ...whole night? Yes if that's what you want and you've got the money mister *(beat)* My name? Not important...call me whatever you like. *(the boy smiles and then walks as if he is getting into a car then exits stage right. Man enters stage left followed after a short time by Lisa.)*

Man I see that kid here almost every night. He always gets into a different car. *(to Lisa)* You notice that? *(Lisa shrugs and smiles)* It's not right. I'm telling you something's not right there. I's got a bad feeling with that kid. *(Lisa shrugs again, she is nervous and unsure how to respond to the man)* Cat got your tongue?

Lisa No speak English. Little English.

Man No one speaks English these days. I swear you'd think you were living in some foreign country half the time. *(starts a racist rant about people bleeding the system, getting benefits etc.)* Where you from then?

Lisa No English. *(speaks in a foreign language)*

Man I was born here you know. British citizen. Don't help me though, not one bit. I mean you'd think it'd be easy like being born here and all, but people is racist here. Don't

	like the colour of your skin, your hair. You knows what I mean? You know sometimes I wish I didn't speak English neither. *(Lisa shrugs and smiles)* Country? Where you come from? *(he is speaking loudly and slowly as if this will make her understand better, she flinches at the raised voice)* Wow, calm down. What the hell's your problem.?*(Anna walks to the bus stop. She looks at the man, nods, looks at Lisa)*
Anna	What's gotten into her?
Man	Don't ask me. How the hell would I know?
Anna	You okay there? *(Lisa looks frightened, speaks in foreign language for a few sentences)*
Man	She don't speak English.
Lisa	Little English. *(speaks in a foreign language)*
Anna	What the hell! Nobody speaks bloody English around here.
Man	*(laughing)* Was just sayin' the same thing!
Anna	So where you from?
Man	*(without giving Anna a chance to speak)* Me? Me? What you mean where am I from? Cos I'm black you think I can't be from here – this country's full of fuckin racists you know, racists and fuckin foreigners! *(in her face)* I'm from the streets, the land of the revolution, the land of …….. *(continues at length in a style that fits his poetical philosophical style)*

Anna	Idiot! Course I know where you're from. *(to Lisa)* Where are *you* from?
Man	Already asked her. I told you she don't speak no English!
Anna	*(persistent, slow and very loud)* Where are you from?
Man	She aint deaf or special needs for fuck's sake. I said she don't speak no English.
Anna	*(irritated and persistent)* Well she must know some English. She knows this is a bus stop doesn't she!
Lisa	Bus, yes bus.
Anna	See! You speak English then don't you.
Lisa	Little English. *(speaks in foreign language, then she eyes the audience suspiciously and finally speaks to them)* I am like many girls…many have same situation. I am not the only one. There are many like me. Man come to my village. He has big expensive car, nice clothes. He was so polite, friendly. He take me drink soda and buy me burger. He spoke of famous cities he often visited. Rome, London, Paris, Madrid and many other ones, I could only dream about. He tell me I beautiful girl - in his country I can be model. He said he work for modelling agency that looks for pretty girls like me. My face become very red but I like to hear these things. He come to house talk to parents. My father not so happy but I beg him and I cry he let me go be famous model. He agree but not happy. Man come next day to take me to be model. I say

	goodbye to family. Probably they think I dead now. I hope so. It is easier than truth. *(beat)* I have done things they never can imagine. *(beat)* I can never see them again.
Anna	*(to man)* Let's have some fun with this one *(signalling Lisa)* Nothing else to do round here tonight. *(to Lisa)* Hey you? *(Lisa looks questioningly)* Yeh you. We'll help you learn some English. Speak then. *(Lisa shrugs, Anna bored and persistent)* Speak English. You can speak English! Show me. What can you say in English?
Man	*(cynically)* You're wastin' your time with that one.
Anna	Shut up! Come on speak some more. Speak English.
Lisa	I know say *(beat)* 'how much?'
Man	*(man and Anna looking at one another)* What the ….? *(Man and Anna laugh)*
Anna	*(deliberately encouraging her)* Yeh that's it, you're doing great, tell us some more.
Lisa	*(feeling encouraged as she misreads their laughter)* They teach me say 'you like, I do with hand, mouth, special price *(pleased by their supportive reaction)*… for good price I swallow…'
Man	*(cuts her off)* Wow! Stop right there. *(Anna and the man look at one another)* I only just met you! *(laughing)* That's some English she's got! They don't teach that at no school I went to. If they had I'd be

	having hundred percent attendance! Man! What are you on?
Lisa	*(worried)* I say bad? *(speaks in foreign language for a few sentences)*
Man	*(laughing sarcastically)* Well I suppose that depends on who you ask. I knows a couple of brothers who might take you up on that. All depends on what that special price is.
Lisa	*(worried)* I say bad? *(speaks in foreign language for a few sentences)*
Anna	Well I think we know where she learned her English.
Man	*(checking Lisa up and down)* Too right! I think we all know.
Lisa	We drove some hours to the coast. *(beat)* He had new passport but told me he must keep it so it be safe. It was first time I saw sea and first time in ship. It seemed very big and beautiful. We meet three other girls and he tell me they will be models too. *(beat)* I jealous I not only one. *(beat)* We go into ship and down many stairs - smell of oil was very strong, smell of rotten food and clothes not washed in long time. Man say for our safety he must lock door but will return in morning. He say he take care of us very good. He say we girls must share bed, but only one night and next day we arrive! *(beat)* Sound of engine was very loud and soon ship moving very fast. *(beat)* We talk about handsome men we going to meet and how girls at home be jealous.

	(beat) We happy but bad smells and moving ship make us very sick.
Anna	*(concerned about Lisa)* You in trouble hun?
Lisa	*(worried and defensive)* I no trouble. I good girl.
Anna	It's okay *(calming Lisa)* I know. I know. I think you and me speak the same language. *(laughs ironically)* We're more alike than you know. *(Lisa smiles)*
Lisa	I good girl *(speaks in foreign language for a few sentences)*
Anna	Yeh sure you're a good girl. You're a very good girl. And I'm a good girl too. *(man laughs and Anna throws him a dirty look)* We're all good girls. At least we were…once. *(remembering, speaking to audience, other characters oblivious to these thinking out loud moments)* You know they say I was fortunate. Figure that! Fortunate! *(beat)* I was abducted when I was fifteen. *(beat)* Oh my parents organized a search and everyone came to help. All the neighbours, even strangers…well that's what they told me. *(beat)* They found me three days later…by accident. My mum said it was luck they found me. Luck! If I was really lucky I'd be dead. *(beat)* I was in his car outside this garage and someone recognised me. Called the police. *(beat)* You know they never did catch him. *(beat)* You think something like

	that could never happen to you, you know that it only happens to other people.
Man	It's a cold one tonight. *(looks to Lisa who smiles confused)* Cold I said. You know…cold! *(Man mimes being cold, Lisa nods)*
Lisa	Cold.
Man	*(to Anna)* You hear that. I is teaching her some English.
Anna	*(sarcastically)* Yeh you're a regular teacher. Missed your calling you did.
Man	Damn right I did! *(to Lisa, inviting her to sit down with him at the bus stop)* I got some pure lessons here, everything you need is in this paper. Look at this, okay see this word x-factor, yeh you know x-factor *(Lisa repeats)* well like me I got the x-factor *(Lisa repeats)*. That's it you's doing good here. Let's try a new one… celebrity, I know it's a long one, difficult but try, ce-leb-ri-ty, like me I'm a celebrity, local celebrity, everyone around here knows who I am, even the police. *(Anna attempts to say it but can't)* Okay okay don't be stressing these are some big words. What about this… this is a good one 'Jimmy Saville'… *(she repeats, man laughs)*
Anna	*(to audience)* You know I was a typical teenager, always fighting with my parents, liking boys, music, dancing…. *(trails off as if remembering with a smile)*. I started hanging around with a new group of friends at school. Jane was in that group –

	she was the pretty one, popular with all the boys. We became best friends. She was always inviting me for a sleepover. But my mum would never let me go. *(beat)* I hated her for that. *(beat)* I hated her cos all my friends would go and I'd always be the one not allowed *(beat)* so I kept hassling my mum and eventually she said ok. *)* My mum had met Jane, she'd even met her dad *(beat)* she even called to check up that we were really having a sleepover and not lying so we could go out. *(the boy wanders back on stage but stays in the shadows)*
Man	*(noticing the boy, speaking to Anna)* I'm telling you that kid's a strange one.
Anna	Something not right there that's what I say.
Man	Out alone this time of night. He's just a kid. *(beat)* Kids today, they grow up too fast. You know I was just saying the other day that… *(another philosophical rant about young people nowadays and values etc)*
Anna	Sometimes kids have no choice *(man and Anna exchange a knowing look)* Know what I mean?
Man	You think I don't know that! *(man nods, uncomfortable silence follows then Anna continues to audience)*
Anna	Sometimes – most of the time – I think it would have been better if they had never found me *(beat)* if I had died. *(beat)* Sometimes I used to look at my mum and

	I'd like catch her watching me…and I knew she was thinking the same thing.
Man	*(to Anna)* You work around here?
Anna	*(laughing ironically)* You could say that. *(aggressively)* What's it to you?
Man	I was only trying to make some polite fuckin conversation. Art of conversation's dead around her man. Shit!
Anna	*(continuing with her memory to audience)* But Jane's dad wasn't really her dad *(beat)* and she wasn't really fifteen. *(beat)* He had a record for having sex with underage girls. *(beat)* Maybe Jane was one of them, but I don't understand why she would help him then. I mean, why would she help him hurt other girls like her? *(beat)* Her dad took us to this house and said he'd be right back … he just left us there. *(beat)* I asked Jane for a drink and she brought me some coke. *(beat)* I drank it and then I just blacked out. *(beat)* When I woke up, I felt kind of sick and groggy *(beat)* I couldn't move.
Man	*(moving closer to Lisa)* You want something – something to make you feel better, make you forget? I got stuff you know?
Lisa	*(scared but desperate)* You help me? *(speaks in a foreign language)*
Man	I got stuff to help you.
Anna	*(seeing what the man is trying to do)* Oh for fuck's sake!

Man	Yeh I got some *(clearing his throat and lowering his voice)* drugs, you know.
Lisa	Help yes help!
Man	Wow keep your voice down. Shit man!
Lisa	*(to audience)* The next morning we arrive and he take us to house where streets are dirty, many people begging ... rats. We did not expect this. In this place was girl's magazines, bad ones, bottles, cigarettes on floor. *(beat)* Some men sitting inside, they laugh and look at us in bad way. I ask him who they are, but he grab my arm and say something very bad. He hit me on face. He pull me by hair into room and hit me. *(beat)* I do not understand. I hear other girls screaming. *(beat)* Then he rape me. *(beat)* Other men come do same. *(beat)* Each day same men comes again, then others. *(beat)* If I say no, they beat me and give me no food. He said *this* is modelling we must do this modelling for anyone he say. If I say no he give me drugs. I see other girls take many drugs. If you take the drugs you don't fight back. Drugs make you like dead person. You see, you hear but you stop to feel.
Anna	*(to the man)* What the hell you trying to do?
Lisa	Help? You help. I good girl. *(speaks in foreign language for a few sentences)*
Anna	I asked you what the hell you were doing?
Lisa	Help? You help. I good girl. *(speaks in foreign language for a few sentences)*

Man	Nothing *(beat)* Man this aint worth the agro. *(moving away from Lisa, to Anna)* A job's a job, you pedal where you can.
Anna	*(angry and defensive)* You get away from her. Leave her alone. *(beat)* I know your type. *(as they exchange, Lisa moves back into the shadows and disappears)*
Man	You don't know nothing. *(beat)* Who the fuck do you think you are judging me? *(getting angry)* You don't know shit. *(beat)* Look at you, you think I don't know what you are?
Anna	I know your type! You think I don't know what you're trying to do with her *(as she goes to point at Lisa she notices she's gone)* Where'd she go? *(to audience, remembering again)* Then I looked and tried to really focus. *(beat)* My legs were being held down, and this guy was raping me. *(beat)* I was trying to scream, trying to beg him to stop and leave me alone, but I had no voice. *(beat)* I could hear the words in my head but they were so quiet when I tried to say them out loud. *(beat)* He said I must like it then. *(beat)* There were others there and he told them to come and rape me too. *(beat)* He told them I liked it. *(beat)* 'Look at her smiling' he said. *(beat)* But I wasn't smiling. *(snapping back to reality, turns to the man)* You scared her off you did!
Man	Didn't do nothing man. She was crazy, you heard the way she talked. I'm telling you this place is full of crazies.

Anna Yeh you would know.

Man What's that supposed to mean?

Anna Take it however you want.

Man *(sarcastically)* I bet you say that to all the guys?

Anna *(glares back angry and hurt, starts to speak then stops, walks towards him, pauses)* Fuck you! *(walks back, to audience, remembering again)* I felt so weak, I couldn't fight them off. *(beat)* And I kept blacking out. *(beat)* Every time I woke up I was still being raped. *(beat)* Every single time. *(beat)* Jane's 'dad' took money off the men he gave me to … if I cried or tried to say no he told me he would kill me, then he would go get my little sister and use her instead. *(beat)* Jane knew my sister *(beat)* She was only ten. *(beat)* So I stopped complaining and crying. *(beat)* I stopped asking them to leave me alone. *(beat)* I just wanted to die. *(beat)* I just wanted to die. *(while she has been talking Odette has entered stage right but in the shadows, remains there)*

Odette *(sits half turned to the audience, it is not obvious at this point that she is heavily pregnant)* In my country war came. They kill my family. I see the husband die, the father die, many people die. So much death – you stop to feel. The soldiers take me. They rape me – every day for many weeks. I want only to die. I ask them 'kill me please'. They laugh. I only want to die.

	(beat) I only want to die. I think if I die, all will be good, I will be happy again.
Man	*(approaching Anna)* You know I didn't mean to… *(trails off)* …just been one of them nights. Business is slow. Know what I mean?
Anna	Yeh I know. Every night's one of them nights these days.
Man	We're in a recession like. Read that on the paper. *(starts pontificating about what he has read in the paper seeing himself as an expert in the area – use whatever is topical to the moment)* People just aint buying drugs like they used to.
Anna	People just aint buying nothing like they used to.
Man	True dat! True dat!
Anna	*(smiles weakly, continues to audience)* They did that for three days. *(beat)* I was covered in blood and so dirty. Sometimes they would give me some water to drink but every time I drank it I'd black out *(beat)* when I woke up there were always new men there. When they found me I was very weak. They took me to hospital and they told my parents I had an STD. I was only fifteen and I had an STD. Do you understand? *(beat)* They cleaned the wounds and they got better. *(beat)* They gave me medicine for the STD and it got better. *(beat)* But the sickness it caused in my head *(long pause)* that never goes away. *(beat)* After that you can't ever be

	normal again. I think I became a walking target for predators, pimps, traffickers. You know they have this uncanny radar to seek out damaged children, to force them into trafficking *(looks over at the boy)*. Nobody helped me. *(beat)* Learning to feel like a human again is…well it's…difficult. *(still looking at the boy)*
Odette	The soldiers left me to die but I was not so lucky. I go to hospital then to refugee camp. White man came, good man, and told me I need help. I get headache, bad headache all the time after what soldiers do to me. This man, he tell me he has friend who will bring me to UK where I get help. They will take me to hospital and I get better. I am happy very happy. I think I start new life. *(starts singing gently and continues to do so as others speaks)*
Man	*(to Anna)* Hey you ok, you zoned out there, gone all weird like.
Anna	*(snapping back)* Fine
Man	You on drugs or something?
Anna	*(sarcastically)* The drug of life. That's my drug of choice. I'm high on the drug of life.
Odette	*(singing more loudly)* I dream of a new life. I dream of good things. I know, I think, I will be safe now. *(long pause)* But it was all a lie.
Man	*(at a loss for what to say)* It's cold out tonight.

Anna So you keep sayin' . You got fuckin tourettes or something?

Man No I fuckin aint got fuckin tourettes for fucks sake. Just trying to make some fucking conversation you fuckin bitch! *(boy laughs, man looks at him)* And you can fuck off too!

Anna That kid shouldn't be out so late, not on his own.

Man I knows it. Up to no good probably.

Anna *(cynically)* Well you'd know wouldn't you?

Man *(annoyed)* And what the fuck's that supposed to mean?

Anna *(weary)* Nothing, nothing at all. *(beat)* I know your type that's all.

Man Here we go again. You think you knows my type. I told you lady you don't know shit about me. *(to the boy)* Hey kid who you waiting for?

Boy *(Stepping out from the shadows)* Waiting for my dad.

Man Shit son how many dad's you got? *(laughing)* Looks like you got a new one every night. *(boy shifts uncomfortably)* Waiting for your dad hah! I aint buying that one. *(during the exchange Anna moves stage right and bends down as if talking to someone in a car)*

Boy And I aint selling so mind your own fuckin' business mister.

Man	Mind your fuckin mouth kid.
Boy	I aint no kid.
Man	What's your name?
Boy	What's it to you?
Man	Is it a secret? Or aint you got no name?
Boy	*(annoyed by this wants to say something, searches for a name to say)* Ronaldinho!
Man	*(laughing)* You tellin' me your name's Ronaldinho.
Boy	You got a problem with that?
Man	*(laughing)* Ronald Macdonald more like.
Boy	Fuck off!
Anna	*(to guy in car)* Fifty quid. *(beat)* Okay thirty quid you cheap bastard. *(beat)* What the hell? You want what? *(beat)* Well that'll cost you more then. *(beat)* Just drive round the corner. *(beat)* There's a parking lot round there. *(beat)* Empty at this time. *(moves further stage right as if getting in a car)*
Man	Watch your mouth son!
Boy	I aint your son!
Man	Too right cos if you were I'd give you one of these! *(makes action to slap him)* Seriously, what you sellin' kid?
Boy	What you buyin'?
Man	Listen you little smart ass, all I is saying is this is my place for sellin'…know what I'm sayin'?

Boy (in his face and pushing him back)We aint selling the same thing mister. *(runs off)*

Man Wait! Put your hands on me again kid and you're dead. *(starts after the boy then stops, walks back to bus stop and sits down, agitated)* Who the hell does he think he is and who does she think she is, 'knows my type'. Knows nothing about me. People look and think they know. Let me tell you, they don't know shit about me. *(beat)* You think this just happens, that you just end up pushing drugs on a street corner. *(beat)* I got a family to feed…and I look after my family…I look after my kids…any way I can. *(beat)* I got no choice *(beat)* I never had no choice. *(beat)* That's the kind of dad I had. So don't go judging me. *(beat)* You don't know what it's like, you're eight years old and all you know is if you don't do the deliveries you get the shit beaten out of you. You got to do what you're told. *(beat)* Truth is most times he'd be high and beat the shit out of me anyway. *(beat)* She'd be high too. She was always high. *(beat)* He'd bring guys round for her to…*(trails off)*…to get money for more drugs. They'd put me in the cupboard so I couldn't see nothing *(angry)* but I got ears haven't I? *(beat)* Listenin' to that night after night. *(covers his ears)* Does something to you. Messes with your head. *(Puts his hands over his ears. Maria walks to the bus stop, Man looks up they nod to greet one another).*

Maria	It's a cold one tonight. *(man grins and nods)*
Man	Tell me about it.
Maria	Has the 21 been yet?
Man	You just missed it. *(beat)* Waitin' on the 35 myself.
Maria	Shit.
Man	Seen you before. You're always running for that bus *(beat)* and you're always missing it! *(laughs)* You need to learn to run faster, I'm telling you! Or lose some weight lady!
Maria	*(a mixture of sad and offended)* That's what *he* says. *(beat)* It's my work. I've only got five minutes to get downstairs and across to the bus stop. *(beat)* There's not a bus ever on time in this city except that one. I swear he's even early half the time. I mean it's ridiculous, what bus is ever on time around here? *(beat)* They're not supposed to do that you know? They're not supposed to do that. Leave early I mean.
Man	*(disinterested but polite)* No
Maria	*(caught up in her own conversation, oblivious to the man's disinterest)* And there's not another one for thirty minutes and *he's* always late. Bloody typical. *(beat)* My husband's going to kill me if I'm late again *(long pause)* especially on a Friday. *(beat)* You know yesterday I'm

	sure he saw me running across the road and just as I made it, he drove off. Bastards!
Man	*(suddenly paying attention, sarcastically)* Bus drivers or men in general. *(Maria looks at him properly for the first time, becoming uncomfortable at the 'type' she sees him as, doesn't answer him and starts to move a little further away. Man notices and gets annoyed)* What you think I'm gonna do lady? Rob you?
Maria	*(defensively, clutching her handbag, hesitatingly)* Maybe…
Man	*(moving towards her aggressively as a joke)* Maybe you think I'm gonna rape you?
Maria	*(immediately)* No! No of course not… well maybe…I mean maybe…
Man	*(angry)* Are you for real? You'd be so fuckin lucky! Get real bitch. *(Maria starts to cry a little and moves away slightly)* Oh for fucks sake. *(to audience, getting worked up)* I'd beg her not to put me in the cupboard. She'd tell me to be a good boy, play with my toys. *(beat)* Not to make a sound. *(beat)* Sometimes they'd beat her too and he'd be there watching, doing nothing. *(beat)* Once I came out to stop this guy beating on her. Mum kept telling me to be quiet and get back in the cupboard. I told him to leave her alone and started pulling at him to get him off her. *(beat)* He laughed. Then he got mad and said he wasn't doing it with a kid around

and that she was sick. *(beat)* He left and I ran to her to see if she was okay. She pushed me away and then she started hitting on me over and over again, telling me I'd ruined everything. *(beat)* I kept crying and asking her to stop but she didn't. *(long pause)* After that they made me go outside when men came over. Didn't matter what time it was, or how cold, or how long.... *(trails off looks to the left and sees a bus approaching).* That's me...lucky for you bitch. No? *(gets up then stops briefly and turns back to look at Maria)* Get a life lady. You hear me, get a fuckin life you loser! *(hails the bus and moves off stage right)*

Maria *(shouting after him, indignant)* What's that supposed to mean? Who does he think he is? *(shouting after the bus)* Stone-head! Loser!*(pacing agitated, to audience)* Who's he to call me a loser? I'm not a loser. Look at him...I know his type and *(shouting after him)* you're all losers, every one of you! *(suddenly aware she has been shouting and embarrassed, looks around to make sure nobody is there)* An when I get home he'll be mad cos I'm late again, especially on a Friday. *(beat)* Friday night's poker night. I'm supposed to be there to serve them drinks, you know *(beat)* be the good wife. *(beat)* Sometimes I miss the bus deliberately you know. Well not deliberately but I just don't go as fast as I should, as fast as I could I mean. *(beat)* I know I'll get it when I get back. *(Boy*

189

	appears in the background shadows) I know he'll be mad… but it just delays …delays…it just delays the…*(trying to change the subject of her thoughts, looks around)* the bus is late again *(sees the boy)*. Look at that kid, I just know something's not right but why should I try to help – and he's a rude little shit. People always just think they can be rude to me, that I'm one of those people you can walk all over, but I'm not. I'm telling you I'm not!
Boy	*(approaching Maria)* Got a light lady?
Maria	*(stirring from her thoughts, had not noticed him approach)* What?
Boy	Got a light?
Maria	No I do not! And you should not be smoking at your age. *(looking closer at him)* How old are you anyway? Twelve?
Boy	*(proudly)* Thirteen and a half!
Maria	*(curious and with a sudden tenderness)* What are you doing out alone at night like this son? *(beat)* You okay? *(beat)* You got a home to go to?
Boy	I got a home.
Maria	You got someone to take care of you?
Boy	What's it to you? *(regrets being rude and tries to backtrack)* Yeh I have. *(moves closer to the bus stop)*
Maria	What's your name?
Boy	What's it to you?

Maria	*(hurt)* Just asking. *(beat)* My name's Maria.
Boy	*(feels bad for being rude)* Alex
Maria	That's a nice name.
Boy	*(enjoying the reaction)* Alex Oxlaide-Chamberlain *(Boy moves into bus stop and sits beside her)*
Maria	That's a long name
Boy	You can call me 'the Ox'.
Maria	*(oblivious to the fact that it's a footballer's name, starts fumbling in her bag)* Okay Ox … you hungry?
Boy	Yeh
Maria	*(takes out a sandwich and begins to share it with the boy)* You look hungry. I had a boy – would have been your age if…*(long pause)* stillborn.
Odette	I have a son. In the war he ran with my mother when the soldiers came. I watch him run but the soldiers take me and I never see him again. I think he may be dead. If he is not dead, I think he must hate me. *(beat)* I am a bad mother. *(beat)* I did not save him. *(beat)* one day, one day soon, I will go look for him. Maybe he got to safe place. So long ago now. Maybe he not know who I am. He not recognise my face.
Boy	*(the conversation that follows is slow and spoken between eating)* What's that?
Maria	What's what?
Boy	Stillborn?

Maria	When the baby's born dead.
Boy	Sorry. *(curious, pause)* Did you cry?
Maria	Lots.
Boy	Why'd he die?
Maria	Don't know. Things happen.
Boy	What did the baby's dad say? *(beat)* Did he cry?
Maria	No he didn't cry. *(beat)* He said it was my fault.
Boy	*(eating the sandwich ravenously)* Was it?
Maria	*(looks at him for a while)* No. I don't think so. I hope not.*(looking at the boy)* You were hungry! *(he nods)*
Boy	Yep!
Maria	*(smiling, enjoying talking to the boy and wanting to prolong it)* You want some chocolate *(boy smiles and nods enthusiastically, Maria takes out some chocolate and gives it to him)* You know if you were my boy I wouldn't let you out late at night like this. *(boy engrossed in the food not really listening, Maria continues to audience)* I don't mind them playing poker. I don't even mind serving them drinks, even if they are rude and make such a mess. It's when he loses. That's when…he takes money off them and lets them…well he lets them do stuff, you know, to me, you know what I mean. So he doesn't have to pay them. Sometimes he even sits there watching and he shouts at

me if I cry. He says I should be happy that other men think his wife is attractive. But that's not true. That's not what they're thinking. I know that. It used to just be Fridays but now it's more often. *(emotional)* You know even when I was pregnant he... That's why I'm slow to catch the bus, you know *(beat)* cos sometimes I just don't want to go home.

Boy What?

Maria Sometimes I don't want to go home. *(beat)* Is that why you're here? *(beat)* Do you not want to go home either?

Boy *(engrossed in the chocolate, speaks without thinking letting his guard down)* No I gotta get money or I can't go home. I'm not allowed to go back til I've got 300 quid...

Maria *(shocked)* What?

Boy *(realising he's said more than he should)* Nothing! Nothing! I'm just messing with you lady. *(stands up agitated)* Listen, I gotta go.

Maria Wait, what do you mean you've got to get 300 quid? What....

Boy *(cutting her off)* Thanks for the sandwich and the chocolate. *(starts to run off, then stops and turns back for a moment)* Lady, I'm sorry about your baby *(hesitates then remembers her name)* Maria. *(they both look at one another and smile)* See you tomorrow? *(exits before she can respond)*

Maria	*(stands up and looks after him)* That's not right. It's just not right. But what can I do? I can't even help myself. *(beat)* You know I have a daughter. *(beat)* She lives with his mum. I don't see her much. He says it has to be like that and that if I'm good I can spend time with her. I live for those days. *(beat)* She's so big now. *(beat)* He says it's wrong for a child to be in the same house as me cos of the things I do. But he's the one who makes me do them! He says he has photos and film of it all and if I ever try to run away, he'll show the police and I'll never see my daughter again. Never! *(to the public)* So what choice do I have. *(beat)* So you see I can't be helping that kid cos the police might start asking questions about me and… *(sees her bus coming)* …at last, about bloody time! *(waves at the bus, exits stage right).*
Boy	*(wanders back on stage and walks towards a car, we are hearing one side of the conversation)* You want to be my daddy…. Yes I can stay all night but it will cost you… how long are you here for…three days?…. you gotta pay extra then … and you gotta take me for food…yeh? …Good places like Pizzaexpress, MacDonald's, KFC…yeh you ok with that? … You gotta buy me trainers?...Yeh?...Adidas…we'll go shopping…No it's okay. I'll call you dad. Nobody will ask questions…They never do! *(beat)* Three days, right? *(exits stage right as Lisa enters stage left)*

Lisa	*(speaking in a foreign language and clearly distressed, then continues to audience)* He say he pay for passports and documents. They belong to him and to be without them in foreign country mean go to prison if police find us. If we try escape, he and friends will kill us and no one will ever know. If we succeed and go to police, bad things happen to our families and they will tell everyone we prostitutes. He laugh and say we stupid. He ask what the parents and friends say if they know we prostitutes. I feel so ashamed for what he make us to do.
Anna	*(seeing Lisa)* You again.
Lisa	No English *(speaks in foreign language for a few sentences)*
Anna	Don't start that again. It's like déjà fuckin' vu! *(beat)* See even I'm speaking like a fuckin foreigner now. *(to Lisa)* It's fuckin contagious I'm tellin' you!
Lisa	You help me?
Anna	*(she looks at her for a long time, saddened)* No!
Lisa	*(shocked)* No? *(desperate)* Please?
Anna	*(suddenly angry and starting to shout)* No! No help! Nobody helps anyone. You gotta help yourself.
Lisa	No understand. Little English. Help please? *(Anna turns away, Lisa pleads in a foreign language)*
Anna	*(to audience but in background we hear Lisa pleading in a foreign language and*

Odette singing) We're all for sale one way or another. *(beat)* We just don't all get to choose the price. *(beat)* I remember the staircase that led to the room, I remember it was on the eighth floor of this old building. The hallways were stone, cold stone, every footstep echoed. That was when I realized it was all happening again. *(beat)* Maybe some people just attract it. *(beat)* How can it happen again I thought. *(beat)* There were other girls in the room but nobody looked up. Nobody cared, everyone in their own misery. I was no different. This woman near me, she started crying. *(beat)* I sat down looking at the window, trying to ignore her, block her out like. *(beat)* There was a big bay window at one end of the room and the windows were open. I could hear noises from the street. There were curtains. White chiffon curtains. I remember that. *(beat)* That woman, the one who was crying, she crossed the room stopped at the window then she just jumped. Just like that. Nobody said anything. When she hit the ground, she broke her legs and arms. *(beat)* I looked down at her crying, her body was twisted like a rag doll and I thought, what a shame she didn't die and then I went to sleep.

Odette   In UK he take me to his house. It is small. I say 'you take me to get help for the head'. He tell me 'shut up'. He says this is home now. *(beat)* He says I must clean the house and be his wife. He tell me there is saying where he come from 'the woman who is

	not beaten is like house that is not cleaned'. *(beat)* I make many mistakes because everything is new. I do not understand the cooker or many electric things. *(beat)* He tells me I am ignorant and stupid. *(beat)* He beat me. *(beat)* He tell me I never can go outside. Neighbour must never see me because I have no document, no passport. If neighbour see me they call police and I go prison. *(terrified)* He say if I go prison they will send me back to my country, to the soldiers. He laugh. *(beat)* He say if I shout or scream he cut my tongue and I never talk again. *(beat)* He say I never sing again.
Anna	*(Anna walks up and down touting for business, Lisa is following her speaking a foreign language, reaching out to her)* Get away from me! What's your problem?
Odette	Soon I know I am with child. *(beat)* I tell him. *(beat)* He no speak but I know he is not happy. I see it in the face. He is not happy.
Anna	*(annoyed by Lisa)* Get away from me I said, crazy bitch. You're bad for business. Nobody's going to stop with you hanging on there. I aint no charity.
Lisa	Help. Please.
Anna	*(shouting and pushing Lisa away slightly)* Go away! *(Lisa stops in her tracks)* That's better. *(Lisa steps back into the shadows and disappears)*

Odette	He say nothing. I try many times to speak to him but he say nothing. He tell me not to talk about it. Then time come I know baby is coming and I tell him. *(Anna has continued touting for business and appears to have been successful, exits stage right)* Still he say nothing. *(beat)* I feel baby wanting to come. So much pain. *(beat)* I tell him again. He very angry. He say get in car. *(beat)* I think we go to hospital now. He drive long time. So much pain. I fear baby is coming. Then we stop but it is not hospital *(beat)* it is just street but nobody there. He pull me out of car. I say no and I fall. The pain is so bad from baby coming. *(beat)* He very angry and he pull me telling me I must get out. He leave my lying on ground. *(beat)* It is cold. *(beat)* So much pain. *(beat)* Then he get in car and drive away. *(Odette stumbles into the bus stop holding her stomach and crying out in pain. She falls again and pulls herself to a sitting position leaning on the bench)*
Man	*(entering stage left, sees Odette but she is hunched over so he doesn't realise she is pregnant)* You okay? *(Odette screams in pain)* What the hell! You okay lady? *(she cries and screams again)* You waiting on a bus?
Odette	*(in between expressions of pain and crying)* Bus?
Man	Yeh you're in a bus stop. You waiting on a bus.

Odette	Bus stop? *(Maria and Anna walk on separately stage left)*
Maria	What the hell is wrong with her?
Man	Bad trip I think?
Anna	What'd you do to her?
Man	Didn't do nothing, so don't go accusing me.
Maria	Someone should go check she's okay. *(Maria and Anna step back and man realises he is the only one standing near Odette)*
Man	Why me? Oh no I aint checking. I aint getting the blame for nothing. *(Odette is crying out in pain and starts to speak in a foreign language)*
Maria	What's she saying?
Man	How the fuck would I know? Hear that, she thinks cos I'm black I can speak every fuckin language! *(to Anna about Maria)* Check this one out, the stupid bitch.
Anna	Does nobody in this country speak fuckin' English?
Man	You got something against black people too?
Anna	Only some of them! *(Odette cries again, she pulls herself up on the bench and it is now obvious she is pregnant and in labour)* Oh shit! This aint good!
Man	*(realising what is happening)* Fuck! Someone's gone and filled her up!

	(agitated not sure what to do) Can't you call someone. You got a husband? Fuck fuck fuck! I can't get involved with this. Police will come and I'll get in shit. *(to Odette)* Lady can't you call someone? *(Odette is oblivious to him as the pain worsens)*
Anna	Are you stupid – she's about to give birth in a bus stop and you want her to stop a minute to make a fuckin phone call.
Odette	Bus? Bus… stop… *(cries in pain again)* Help me!
Man	How the hell do I know what she should do? At least I is trying to help.
Anna	Stop trying so hard then!
Maria	Someone's got to do something.
Man	Not me. I was never here.
Anna	Bloody typical. *(beat)* Asshole.
Man	Yeh? Why don't you make the call then!
Anna	*(hesitantly)* I can't be here if the police come. *(man laughs)* I can't get picked up again.
Maria	Picked up…again…what you talking about *(Anna groans at Maria's stupidity).*
Man	*(speaking to Maria as if she's stupid)* She's a whore *(Maria stares back blankly)* You blind lady? How have you survived this long – you aint got a clue. Surprised you can even make it across the road without getting hit by a bloody bus! *(Maria looks at him offended)* Did you just land here from

	another planet? She's a whore *(continues slowly and deliberately)* a prostitute, hooker, lady of the night, joygirl, human trampoline…slut… *(Maria stares back offended)*
Anna	Steady on. *(both getting louder and in each other's faces)* That's rich anyways coming from a drug dealer *(Maria looks shocked)* Seriously? Are you thick or something? Drug dealer! Bagman, candyman, dope peddler, drug trafficker - asshole! *(to Maria)* You get the picture now?
Man	Yeh an' I is in business cos whores like you are buyin' what I'm selling.
Maria	*(raising her voice in anger)* Stop it! Both of you shut up, we gotta help this woman.
Man	What the fuck? When did you grow a pair? Check this out, you know if a woman spoke to me like that normally I'd give her the back of my hand but *(to Anna mocking Maria)* I'm kind of scared of this one that she might do some sumo shit on me. *(Man and Anna laugh)* Listen lady, I aint gotta help no one. I'm outta here.
Maria	But we gotta help her. The baby's coming.
Anna	*(sarcastically)* That baby's gonna be celebrating its fifth birthday at this rate.
Man	That's real helpful!
Anna	*(sarcastically)* I aim to please!
Man	I bet you do. *(Anna courtesies)*
Maria	What we gonna do?

Man	'We' aint gonna do nothing cos 'I' is leaving.
Maria	Look isn't that a police car over there…
Man and Anna	*(cutting her off)* What?
Maria	We can ask them for help!
Anna	I'm outta here now.
Man	Me too! *(both exit)*
Maria	*(looks around unsure what to do, Odette continues screaming in pain)* Come on we gotta get you some help. Always the same I get left to fix everybody else's mess. *(well-intentioned but clumsy, tries to help Odette up, she is doubled over in agony. Lights fade. They exit, lights up on Lisa who enters stage left)*
Lisa	*(speaking in a foreign language, agitated, stops looks at audience, agitated again)* I dreamed of good man to love me. Take care of me. I dreamed of good life in UK. *(beat)* Now who will have me? *(beat)* I'm spoiled. *(beat)* That's what he say. *(beat)* Can never go back home – the shame. Can never run away because police will take me to prison cos I no have documents no passport and he say I whore. He say police put the whore in the prison and she never come out. *(beat)* I just want die. *(beat)* I am young but I look old. I never have children because things they do to me. *(beat)* I not beautiful now. *(head in hands at the side of the bus stop)* I just want to die. *(Man enters followed by Maria and after a little while Anna. They look at Lisa)*

Man	*(to Lisa)* You alright there?
Lisa	No English. *(beat)* Speak little English.
Man	*(groaning)* I knows. Heard it before luv.
Anna	You'd think she'd have bloody learned by now.
Man	Typical bloody foreigner! They're all the same, come here and live off our benefits, do nothing *(to Lisa)* you're all the bloody same!
Lisa	*(getting up and shouting in Anna's face)* No English…speak little English. *(fades into the shadows)*
Man	*(laughing)* That's you told! *(Lisa kicks him as she storms by)* Crazy bitch! *(after a pause, to nobody specific)* It's a cold one tonight. *(the others nod)*
Maria	Hey anyone seen that kid around *(beat)* you know the one who used to hang around the bus stop every night.
Man	Yeh I know the one you mean.
Anna	Yeh cheeky little shit. About twelve years old.
Maria	*(coming in quickly)* Thirteen and a half! *(the others look at her and mimic her, she continues oblivious)* He'd probably be fourteen now.
Man	I aint seen him for months. Probably got himself a new daddy *(laughs)* a rich one.
Anna	You think that's funny. *(the look at one another)*

203

Maria	He was a good kid really.
Man	*(laughing)* Was he fuck!
Maria	His name was Alex?
Anna	That little fucker told me it was Robin, Robin, what was it, Robin Van … van…some foreign shit… van Pissy or Van Persie…something like that…
Man	*(laughing, the only one who realises he has told them all footballer names)* Are you serious? Let me guess Alex…let me see…Oxlade Chamberlain by any chance?
Maria	*(enthusiastically)* That's it yes!
Man	*(mocking)* That's it, yes! You haven't got a clue you stupid bitches. Well he told me it was Ronaldinho…at least that's an improvement on Van Persie, bloody traitor! *(sees his bus approaching, gets up to stop it)* Well ladies I got people to see and places to be. See you around. *(exits)*
Maria	I hope he's okay.
Anna	*(distracted as she looks for business)* Who?
Maria	The kid.
Anna	Course he is. *(beat)* Kids like that know how to survive. *(beat)* Trust me I know.
Maria	But what if something's happened to him? *(beat)* I don't even know his real name.
Anna	Better that way. *(beat)* Better not to think about it. *(sees a car slowing down, ironically)* Time for work. *(walks towards car)* Fifty quid. *(beat)* Well that'll cost you

	more then. *(beat)* Just drive round the corner. *(beat)* There's a parking lot round there. *(beat)* Empty at this time. *(moves further stage right as if getting in a car)*
Maria	*(watches after her go for a while then to audience)* You know I got five minutes to get downstairs and across to the bus stop. *(beat)* There's not a bus ever on time in this city except that one. I swear he's even early half the time. *(beat)* They're not supposed to do that you know? Leave early I mean. And then there's not another one for thirty minutes and *he's* always late. *(beat)* My husband's going to kill me if I'm late again, especially on a Friday. *(beat)* You know yesterday I'm sure that driver saw me running across the road and just as I made it he drove off. *(beat)* Bastard! … *(sees her bus coming)*…at last! *(waves at the bus, exits stage right.)*

Odette walks on stage carrying a child. She sits down at the bus stop and looks down at the child and begins singing.

Lights fade.

The End

Workshop Ideas

Below are discussion points and exercises that can help not only lead us to a better understanding of the play, but also of Applied Theatre and what it involves. In all Applied Theatre and Theatre of the Oppressed exercises, discussion is key. Always allow ample time for discussion after each exercise and explore what has happened.

Discussion questions

1. Discuss the stage elements of the play and what makes it Applied Theatre e.g. set, lights, props etc.
2. The concept of applied plays is not to take sides but simply to tell the story. How do our feelings about each of the characters change throughout and why?
3. Each character is a victim, yet they all often lack empathy towards one another. Discuss.
4. What is the purpose of this play?
5. Which character do you find the least likeable? Why? What can our feelings towards certain characters reveal about us?
6. The set is designed to make an audience feel entrapped. How do you think this is achieved in this play even though the setting is a bus stop in the street where people can come and go freely?
7. Discuss why you think each of these individuals wanted their stories to be told.
8. All the female characters have names but the male characters are referred to as 'man' and 'boy'. Why do you think the playwright did this?
9. What feelings is the writer trying to evoke in the audience and to what end?
10. When the boy is talking to a driver in a car he looks at an audience member directly and speaks his lines.

What is the purpose of performing these scenes in that way and how do you imagine the audience react?

11. The play is indirectly commenting on the general public's choice to be blind to certain things that happen in front of our eyes and turn the other way. Discuss.
12. Moments of humour are key to many applied scripts in order to give the audience a moment of release. Look at the humorous moments in the play and what preceded them. Why was it so important to include humour at those precise moments?
13. When the audience laughs in applied theatre, they become complicit. What do you think is meant by this?
14. It is normal for an Applied Theatre performance to have a discussion time with the audience after the play. What kind of things would you ask if you were an audience member and why?
15. It has been said that Applied Theatre plays with our emotion and our certainties. Discuss in reference to this play.
16. 'We can all identify with at least one of the characters.' Discuss.
17. Discuss the reason a bus stop was chosen as the setting for the play.
18. 'What if the 'man' is the 'boy' grown up! What would that say about our failure as a society?' Discuss.
19. Sold was made into a docufilm for television. At the end a one sentence update was provided on each character. Why does the play avoid doing this?
20. What are the pros and cons of knowing what happened to each of the characters as was provided in the film version?

Applied Theatre Exercises

When doing these exercises it is important to remember that the different stages will often be carried out on different days and do not need to be done in succession. The exercises can be adapted and used for any of the plays.

Please note that in Applied Theatre time should *always* be allocated to discuss and process the exercises after they have been completed.

Change!

The group are seated on chairs in a circle while one person standing in the middle shouts CHANGE. Everyone must change their seat and the person in the middle tries to get to a seat, leaving a new person stuck in the middle. Participants must change to a new seat each time and cannot take one on either side of them.

After this initial warm up, the person in the middle completes a sentence which begins 'I think/believe/feel…' with reference to the play. Anyone who agrees with the statement must change chairs, while the person who made the statement will try to sit on one of the freed-up seats.

Variations:

- The person in the middle makes observations or comments or a judgement about any of the characters.
- The person in the middle completes the sentence 'If I were (name of character) I would have…'
- The person in the middle completes the sentence 'The play shows us / teaches us…'

Wind Up

A topic for discussion is chosen from the play. For example, 'selling drugs is wrong', 'prostitution is a choice'. A group of actors take on the role of each character and mould themselves into a statue representing what they believe to be their character's thoughts on the topic. The concept is they are clockwork people. When tapped this signifies that they are being wound up. As they are wound up, they must exhaust everything they feel this person would say on the issue, talking without stop as they believe that person or type of person would.

When they have exhausted the topic they wind down and come to a stop. They can only speak on the topic again if they are wound up. This exercise often leads to the stereotyping of identities and this is a good point for discussion.

Variation: instead of individuals taking turns, all of the actors can be wound up at the same time to see how the interactions will play out.

The 'bus-stop'

When doing these exercises it is important to remember that the different stages will often be carried out on different days and do not need to be done in succession.

Stage 1: Set up a bench to represent the bus-stop. Play with an exploration of the space and how confining it can be through various exercises:

- Pace the space repeatedly to get a feel for its limiting size

- All characters enter the scene and position themselves within the confines of the bus stop.
- Sit in the space with eyes closed for a lengthy period of time. Explore your senses in the space and how your thoughts begin to wander.

Discuss what you learned about the space; how it made you feel. Imagine that it is a cold, dark winter's night, how would it feel to be waiting in the bus stop?

Stage 2: All characters enter the scene and position themselves within the confines of the bus stop. At a signal from the facilitator they all change position and freeze once again. They hold the position for a couple of minutes before the facilitator signals for them to move again. Each frozen period is time for the actors to reflect on their characters and look at the interaction among the different characters; it also enables a focus on body language and unspoken meaning.

Stage 3: Repeat stage two. This time the actors freeze for 1-2 minutes then, on a signal from the facilitator they begin a dialogue with one another, remaining frozen throughout. Engaging with one another, the actors speak for a few minutes. On a signal from the facilitator they stop speaking and move to a new position and the process is repeated. Always ensure on first moving to the new position, the actors remain frozen for a couple of minutes to gather their thoughts and contemplate their new position. Discuss the process afterwards.

Stage 4: Repeat stage 3. In this stage when the actors begin their dialogue, they are now free to move within the confines of the set (that is, the bus stop). On a signal from the facilitator, the actors freeze again. They contemplate, over a few minutes, what has happened, what was said and the position they currently hold. On a further signal from the facilitator the actors move to a new position and repeat the entire process. Each new position should be influenced by what has gone before and the contemplative time the actors have had. Afterwards discuss the nature of image and the spoken word.

What I see when I look at you

Throughout this exercise it is essential that the actors are in character and respond and speak ONLY as those characters.

Stage 1: The actors in character stand in a circle. One walks to another and gives them a word to describe them in their character's opinion. After giving them the word, they swap places and the actor who received the word now walks to another and does the same and so on. Allow sufficient time for this exercise to ensure the actors exhaust the more superficial and simple words. Actors can return to people they have been to before but cannot use the same word twice with them.

A variation is that the actor receiving the word can refuse to accept it if they feel it does not describe them. They do not speak but they simply refuse to move. The actor using the word can either try a new word and/or move to another character.

Stage 2: The actors remain in the circle. One walks to another makes a statement about the other's character (for example, one might say to Maria 'I don't understand why you stay with your husband'). The other actor responds in one sentence and then they swap places. There is no further exchange than a single statement and response.

The actor who received the statement and responded to it, now walks to another and does the same and so on. Actors can return to people they have been to before but always with a new statement.

Stage 3: Repeat stage 2 only now a question is asked and answered rather than a statement and response. For example, one might ask Maria, 'Why did you not help the boy?; another might ask Odette, 'Do you love your baby?'

The actor who received the statement and responded to it, now walks to another and does the same and so on. Actors can return to people they have been to before but always with a new question.

Stage 4: Discuss the exercise and how it felt to hear the words, statements and questions. Look at why some statements and questions may have been more difficult to answer than others. Have you learned anything new about the characters?

The Worst Case

Throughout this exercise it is essential that the actors are in character and respond and speak ONLY as those characters.

Stage 1: The actors sit in a circle in character. They debate among themselves who has the worst situation. Explore how they react to one another, alliances that are formed; who do they 'gang up' on, or try to protect, or are they only interested in themselves?

This exercise explores the lack of empathy the characters have for one another at times in the play. It would be natural to imagine that they would unite as they are all suffering, but the evidence of the play shows them united at times, but quick to turn on one another also.

Stage 2: One of the actors is removed from the circle. The others then discuss how they feel about him or her. The character who was removed sits outside the circle listening but cannot interrupt or intervene in any way, nor can s/he defend themselves if they feel information is put forward that is untrue or inaccurate. After some time, the actor returns to the circle and another steps out.

Those in the circle now discuss the latest character to have left the circle. The exercise continues until all have been discussed.

After all characters have been discussed, all the actors sit in the circle and can now challenge one another about what they heard said about themselves. The discussion can become quite loud and aggressive but all must remain in their seats throughout. No physical contact is allowed at any point.

Past present future

Stage 1: An actor takes on the role of one of the characters. They then make an image from their character's past using others as needed. When the image is complete, they insert themselves as themselves into the image. The image is held for a few moments. Another actor then comes and replaces the character whose image it is. In this way the character can now look at the image from the outside, looking at themselves in the process.

Stage 2: The character who has stepped out of the image now walks around the image exploring it. S/he taps an individual in the image and that person begins to speak their interior monologue aloud, describing what they believe is going on in their mind as whoever they interpret they are in the image. When they are tapped a second time, they become silent. Throughout, those in the image including anyone delivering their interior monologue must remain still. The character whose image it is moves on to tap another and so on, going back and forth as they see fit. They can also tap the person who represents them.

As each delivers their interior monologues, they are building up an interpretation of the image and who they are within it. Allow sufficient time to build this.

Stage 3: The actor who stepped out of the image now takes a seat. The actors remain still but now can have a dialogue among themselves. Allow this to develop over a period of time. The actor who is not in the image cannot interrupt or correct if s/he feels they have interpreted the image different from his/her attention. Rather they should look at why this interpretation may have happened.

Stage 4: Repeat stages 1 to 3 for a present memory.

Stage 5: Repeat stages 1-3 for an image of the future that awaits the character.

Stage 6: Discuss what has developed and been revealed by the exercise. Has it changed out view of the character in any way? Why/why not?

Inside Out

Inside Out is an Applied Theatre play based on the real-life experiences of people who have experienced homelessness and incarceration. It was created using Applied Theatre and Theatre of the Oppressed techniques throughout.

Each scene reflects a different stage in the seven stages of grief, looking at how the experience of grief and loss is similar. We are never told why **Man 1** was incarcerated or why **Man 2** became homeless to emphasise that both are *'everyman'*.

The play contains strong language throughout.

Both men are seated facing the audience, there is no stage set and there are no props. The stripped-down bare stage is essential to the storyline.

Man 1 – middle aged, hardened and quick to lose his temper. Image is important to him so he likes to be seen in what he considers to be expensive designer sportswear (though all will be fake), especially on his feet.

Man 2 – middle aged but looks older than his years. Wearing mismatched, worn clothing, his shoes will be damaged. His hair unkempt and he will be unshaven.

Scene 1: *shock and denial*

Man 1: Prison smells like shit. Actually it smells worse than shit. (to audience) Imagine shit being rubbed on the armpits of a big fat sweaty bloke and then his armpit and pubes being set on fire too. It's that bad! (pause) No one flushes the shitter. Ever. (to audience) You know how clean prison looks in all the films? That's cos we spend all fucking day cleaning it. And then the inmates just basically shit themselves anywhere and everywhere for a laugh. I don't think there' been a week since I been in here that someone didn't fuck around with their faeces. (pause) Not much else to do I guess.

Man 2: The smells. Your sense of smell changes....sharpens. Smells change. Sitting in the street nowhere to go...every person walking by, smell of a perfume, smell of a bacon butty, coffee, even rubbish, cigarette smoke, the smell of warmth, the smell of homeliness...never thought homeliness had a smell before til I'd lost any sense of what home fuckin was. You smell everything you can ...probably look like a fuckin pervert sometimes sniffing around. My first week...the smell of petrol...a smell I'll never forget...I was sleeping rough and someone tipped petrol over me - set me alight in my sleeping bag. You never forget that...the smell... and then the laughter and the fact that nobody came to help. (long pause) Things to do. Filling time. Time.

	Thinking. Trying not to think. Wish I'd listened to all that meditation shit about emptying my mind. Need to empty my mind. Need to stop thinking. Free time's my enemy.
Man 1:	How the fuck did I end up here! This should never have happened.
Man 2:	How the fuck did I end up here? You tell me – sitting there like you know it all. I own 25p – what the fuck can you buy for 25p these days? *(pause)* Five fuckin plastic bags. I don't even have enough for a bag for life, how ironic, just five shitty plastic bags. I own a battered beat up old holdall and inside's a jumper, a pair of trousers, a pair of shoes and a top hat. (looks at audience) I don't know why the fuck I've got a top hat. Don't even know where the fuck I got it. And believe me it aint much fuckin use to anyone. But it's mine. It's mine, you know what I'm saying? It's mine. I can't throw it away.
Man 1:	You're constantly reminded… inside you own nothing (pause) only things the boss allows you to keep for a time of his choosing. Some people truly have nothing. Just the clothes on their back. Others have whole stockpiles of books and appliances. You can have whatever you can get away with (pause) dependent on your behaviour, your ability to protect it from theft, and your ability to share it with your cellmate. (slowly) I takes stock of my possessions

every day, count them, touch them, arrange them on my shelf. I basically got a square half-foot of space to store things on. Apart from my clothes, I got a small electric razor. The screws prefer it if you have an electric razor – they're harder to kill anyone with. (direct to audience) Not impossible mind – but harder. I mean let's face it if you're mind's set on it you can kill anyone with anything. There was a bible in the cell – left by the poor sod that was there before me I guess. That or the Gideon's have moved their business from hotels to prisons. More chance they'll be read or hoping less chance you'll top yourself. Captive audience and all that. (laughs) I got a few photos - my parents – fuck knows why, my ex fuck knows why and my daughter when she was just born…(pause) oh and I've inherited a mug and a spoon with a hole drilled through it….

Man 2: I found this magazine and it had an article about 'extreme homelessness' like homelessness is an extreme fuckin sport or something. So I thinks, this might be useful…get some tips…and I had nothing fuckin better to do. It was about this old homeless woman in Japan who lived in this guy's cupboard undetected for a year. On the top shelf! A fuckin year! On the top fuckin shelf! And I'm thinking, I couldn't even fit in someone's fucking cupboard never mind hiding on a shelf in it for a year. Seriously what kinda thick bastard didn't realise some old woman's hiding in his

221

cupboard? And I gets kinda obsessed about it, thinking about how she did it. How the fuck she got up on that shelf, how did he not see her...

Man 1: The mug says 'world's greatest dad' – fuckin ironical that is.

Man 2: There was another story about a homeless guy who lived in Heathrow airport for 4 years and only got found out when he bumped into his mam who'd just got off a flight from Majorca and spotted him. Thought about trying this, I mean it'd be warm, open 24 hours, lots of food gets turfed from the cafes, comfy seats, lots of other bastards sleeping on the chairs so you wouldn't look out of place. But you know I think it'd do my head in knowing everyone else had somewhere to go, to know I had no destination, watching people going on holiday, or coming back, business men busy with their business ...it'd just be a reminder every second of the day....would wreck my head it would. I'm obsessed with this 'extreme homelessness' now – no one ends up homeless in the fuckin streets, they're like the 'super' homeless. They make it sound like it's fuckin cool.

Man 1: I shouldn't be here. I did nothing. Nothing! So you (at audience member) take your fuckin judgement elsewhere. (pause) we're all innocent, every fucker I ever met in jail claimed he was innocent I'm telling you (pause) well at first anyway.

Man 2: You don't just wake up homeless one day. So don't you (at audience member) be looking at me and think you know my story cos you don't know shit.

Man 1: Adapting to prison regime is a fucker - whole new set of rules and regulations, whole new set of behaviour norms, respective routines, social hierarchies, different language. Fuck. Overcrowding, frustrating and irritating levels of noise and distraction and little personal space or privacy. Difficult to sleep properly, radios blaring, bars rattling, loud arguments... And then you learn to wait...wait for a phone call, a shower, a meal, the answer to a question even the time of day... waiting and waiting, queuing and queuing. Time gets all distorted, days slip by but every hour's an eternity.

Man 2: You can get used to anything ... if you have to. Know what I'm saying? Remove options, choices and you adapt. (pause)What the fuck else you gonna do?

Man 1: You try and find out as much as you possibly can about the prison you're being sent to... you worry about what the other prisoners will be like, if you'll fit in...it's like being back at bloody school. You're wondering how much stuff can I take with me? Will I be on my own or sharing? Then you arrive and different questions hit you: where do I go to eat, to shower, where is everything…and the worst one… what the fuck have I done to myself?

Man 2: Every day you have questions that go round and round in your head. Where will I get food, where can I clean up, where will I sleep tonight…you go to train stations, public toilets…you want to look smart and not like the stereotype homeless person you think everyone sees, your constantly fighting your own fuckin label.

Man 1: What's the worst thing about first going into prison you may be asking yourself? Probably the lottery you face on arrival. What's your new cellmate going to be like? Will he be a serial killer or an unpredictable psychopath, or will he be some poor bastard suffering from some kind of mental illness who really should be in a loony bin? Don't know which is worse. And if you're really unlucky, you could be bunking up with a big bull homo on the prowl for fresh meat… (to an audience member)I aint no 'gay for the stay' fucker so don't be looking at me like that! In my first week I was threatened with everything from the punishment block to the psychiatric wing and put in a cell with one guy in for murder and another for manslaughter.

Man 2: The shit that comes with being homeless (pause) wouldn't know where to start with that one. The fact that that fuckin label defines you for everyone. The fact that it doesn't take much to end up homeless in the first place. Sounds crazy but people expect some huge long drawn out tragic story, but truth is it can happen to anyone and so quickly, almost creeps up on you like.

Man 1: Everyone asks 'what you in for'. I do a little dance around it, I ask him what he's in for, he doesn't tell me, I tell him one of my charges, he tells me one of his and on and on. And then we both end up bitching about the criminal justice system. You see that's one thing we've all got in common – we've all been fucked over by the system...

Man 2: One of the worst things is just how much *time* I've got on my hands. No TV, no Internet, no video games, no inviting friends round to hang out and just have some damn company. So ... what the hell do you do? (to audience) You tell me! Go to the library – well that works til they realise nobody sits round reading books all day anymore so you gotta be homeless and they move you on. Visit the park and freeze your fuckin balls off or be accused of being a perv....

Man 1: No one, I mean no one is a total asshole to their cellmate. You'd have to be trippin' to do that. Even the biggest asshole inside will still show a degree of respect to the person they're locked up with - you don't want bad blood in the cell unless you want to sleep with one eye open.

Man 2: Sleeping rough you sleep with one eye open all the time. Nowhere to protect your belongings. Nowhere to clean up. Knowing you might get jumped, robbed... or worse...

Man 1: I got challenged by other prisoners, it's a test. I know so long as I stand my ground it'll usually pass without incident. Backing down's just gonna leave me wide open for trouble if they think I'm an easy target. They can smell fear on people – like animals.

Man 2: It's pretty similar to school playground philosophy really. But do they teach you that? Fuck no!

Man 1: I gets told, tie up loose ends before you get sent down, get your business in order, say your goodbyes, get some books. Fuckin books.

Man 2: (angry) What I needed was to be told what to do to not get the crap beaten out of me every fuckin day and for no fuckin reason whatsoever.

Man 1: I was sent to a low security prison ... more freedom of movement, greater privileges...yeh and much less privacy... and much more fuckin dangerous as well ... harder to avoid conflict if it kicks off.

Man 2: And it always kicks off – sooner or later.

Man 1: Humanity counts for little cos to the prison staff, we're just cattle, a number. In the beginning, I tried telling myself, this is

	okay, it's only for a short time, at least I'm on my own, nobody from the outside to give me grief. I kind of thought I'd enjoy being alone. Naïve fuckin bastard.
Man 2:	Only you're never on your own. Surrounded by people yet the loneliness is killing you at times. Whole thing's screwed up.
Man 1:	I wanked off a lot. I read the bible…was the only book I had.
Man 2:	Then I began to imagine I'd been forgotten,
Man 1:	…that everyone on the outside would forget who I was
Man 2:	…and I started to panic.
Man 1:	Once you start down the road, there's no going back.
Man 2:	You think you can handle it, like being alone isn't so bad, like it's almost a relief…
Man 1:	But the cell starts to feel that bit too small.
Man 2:	You lose all track of time.
Man 1:	You can't see the light properly or figure out what time of day it is. You can't distract yourself no more and you start pacing but there ain't enough room to pace proper like and that just makes it worse.
Man 2:	I'd never had a panic attack before, so I didn't know what to expect. My heart just

	started pounding out of my chest and I felt like I was going to faint.
Man 1:	I wanted to faint, so I could at least sleep and waste some fuckin time. But I couldn't (pause) On the plus side, I now have scary accurate recall of obscure biblical passages.

Scene 2: *pain and guilt*

Man 1:	The shock wears off after a while, routine sets in and instead all you get is this excruciating, unbearable pain.
Man 2:	The fear and disillusionment are almost paralyzing. How the hell did this happen to me? I had plans. My life was going somewhere.
Man 1:	Was it fuck! But that's what you tell yourself ain't it.
Man 2:	I sure as fuck didn't plan to end up here. I didn't plan any of this shit. Now I can't plan anything. Do you know what that's like? To never ever be able to plan anything?
Man 1:	To punish myself I thought I wanted to feel that pain, not hide it, avoid it or escape from it with you know like alcohol or drugs.
Man 2:	It was as if the more I could force myself to feel the pain then eventually I'd stop feeling altogether.
Man 1:	I felt guilty but didn't even know what the fuck for anymore, for the things I did…

Man 2: For the things I didn't do. Guilt and regret every moment of every endless fuckin day…

Man 1: …every moment of every endless fuckin night lying awake, trying to force myself to sleep so the time will pass faster. (long pause) I have no regrets, none. I'm telling you, I've worked through my pain, regret and sadness. Tirelessly. I don't need counselling. I don't need no bastard telling me how to feel or think.

Man 2: Counselling isn't going to get me a job is it? It's not going to find me a house. They keep telling me I need to deal with my pain but I'd deal with it a lot better with a fuckin roof over my head! (pause) When you first start sleeping rough, you're afraid of everything and everyone. The reality is a lot easier than the fears … you start meeting others in the same situation and you realise most of them are just ordinary enough people with unfortunate circumstances.

Man 1: You realise the other inmates aren't the social monsters the government and media would have you believe. Well, obviously there are some fuckin psychos in here, but they ain't that common honest and let's face it there's plenty of fuckin psychos on the outside as well! Just look around!

Man 2: Homelessness and addiction – the perennial Catch 22. It numbs the pain. Helps you deal with the cold. Which comes first – the homelessness or the addiction? I mean when you're freezing, when every day of nothingness stretches out in front of you endlessly, when you can't get a job cos you're homeless but you're homeless cos you can't get a job. Fuck! You take the drugs to get through the day, time moves faster, you forget…temporarily…you take the drugs cos what the fuck else can you do? You tell me?

Man 1: Drugs. If you can get them on the outside, you can get them inside and for a better price strangely enough. That is if it's what your man says it is and who the fuck knows … sometimes I swear I was getting high on fuckin jenkem. (pause) Jenkem is the master drug of the new era you know. The working-class man's drug (laughs). It's shit man. No, I mean it – it's shit! Your own shit and piss, mix it together, ferment it for a week or so – (acting out inhaling) inhale and … you can hear your dead relatives and see the future. Jenkem was my logic in this insane world. You should try it. Cheapest drug known to man. Turn off your mind! (pause) Better still get a shot of horse - a hit of that in solitary can make a week pass in no time at all with that stuff. Problem is the shit it might've been cut with. Flour, baking soda, jelly crystals - all shit that shouldn't be in a vein.

Man 2: After a while, you just end up doing things that you never would've dreamed of. Problem is the drugs block out all the cold and the pain and everything else.

230

Everything. So if you get sick you don't even realise. Last year I nearly died of pneumonia ... couldn't catch my breath, fever, headaches... Couldn't move. Couldn't go to a doctor cos I had no ID or address. Blacked out and got rushed to hospital.

Man 1: Codeine tablets. Grew my thumb nail long and wrecked it on the concrete so it was sharp enough to cut open my thigh and would stick the crushed-up tablet inside. Yeah, shit got that bad. Just didn't want to be thinking no more, you know? The number one crime keeping people inside is drugs and most guys learn more about drug crime from TV than they do inside.

Man 2: You become incredibly resourceful. I didn't tell the hospital about the drugs, or that I was homeless. (pause) I was ashamed. I thought they'd throw me out. (pause) Homelessness hurts – in every fuckin way imaginable.

Man 1: The food in here – man it's shit!

Man 2: You eat what you can, where you can. No nutritional value. Unhealthy.

Man 1: Everything inside is about limiting the aggression of prisoners. If they could get away with it, we'd get a shot of Valium every morning and every night. They serve up food that doesn't piss people off and in fuckin big ass portions so we get full, happy ... and, you know, unlikely to start fights.

Man 2: You go days without food, you eat scraps you find, food left by others, go in bins, check alleys behind cafes, restaurants, supermarkets – so long as you don't get seen and moved on you can get some okay stuff. Sometimes it's starting to go off at times but what the hell you going to do? Complain? Call for the chef. (laughs) Worst is when the maggots have started growing in it and you gotta pick them out.

Man 1: Prison food. Three meals a day. It aint easy I'm telling you. Goal is to keep us more interested in food than each other to avoid confrontations. Breakfast sucks, it's always porridge, beans, toast and crappy cheap cereal that never tastes quite right. Milk's always powdered and stored in a big dispenser labelled 'Fresh Milk'. We also get orange juice, only it has no oranges in it. It's a fuckin disgrace I'm telling you. You only go to breakfast if you got no food of your own stashed…oh except for Wednesdays, where there might be powdered eggs and bacon. I kind of like the powdered eggs, they're like the ones you get at McDonalds.

Man 2: You'll eat anything if you're hungry enough. You know this guy stopped in front of me the other day and says 'you expect me to believe you're starving, a fat bastard like you!' I looked at him, had all this stuff I wanted to say but didn't say a word, got no fight left in me for assholes like that. (angrily) What gives someone the right? I don't comment on them and their lives so what fuckin right do they have to comment on mine?

Man 1: Lunch is rarely attended by anyone and's almost always crap for sandwiches. The junkies go to lunch to hoard bread, it's an excellent filter for smack, since cotton balls are impossible to come by. You let the bread start to go a bit dry, then you make little balls from it and put them over your plunger. When you suck the smack into the plunger, the impurities get caught in the bread. Then you ball the bread back up and stash it with the rest of your food. Then if you're without drugs you can suck on the bread balls. (pause) Or you could suck on some other balls and get a new stash. (laughs)

Man 2: You take drugs to stop the cold. You take drugs to stop the hunger. You take drugs to pass the time. You take drugs so you don't think. You take drugs so it all just stops! (pause) You have such a sense of failure and defeat, isolation and self-loathing.

Man 1: Dinner's the same every night. I mean for fucks sake a bit of variety wouldn't kill them would it? Fried chicken... thing was a fryer is considered a brutal weapon, so it's fried off-site and shipped in to be reheated in giant microwaves. So it's soggy as hell. Then pizzas - these fuckers are huge, industrial size. Corrugated cardboard on the underside, with ketchup and cheese. Gives you heartburn for a week. Endless mounds of melted, processed cheese. One of the pizzas always has pepperoni… only I knows it isn't really pepperoni. Fuck if I know what it actually is! Each day the pizzas are laid out in a different pattern. They do that to mess with my head cos I started thinking I could tell the future based on the direction the pepperoni pizza was pointed. Tried to work out what would happen to me, who'd come and visit…

Man 2: Sometimes I'd look at food that'd be thrown away and imagine there was a hidden message, a message to tell me how to turn my life around from some supreme being who couldn't think of a better way to get through to me than ketchup stains and half eaten chips! The meaning of life etched in thrown away food and drunken vomit!

Man 1: Then there's two giant trays of some other shit, an unknown sauce, covered in flat, yellow soggy 'chips'. Basically it all tastes the same. A giant tray of powdered mash, a pot of gravy, occasionally accompanied by a roast of some description on holidays. Then processed fruit, that tastes like plastic. (pause) Sugar. Salt. Fat. That's the key to a safe and happy correctional facility.

Man 2: I have a kid. He doesn't know me. What can I offer him? He's better off without me. His mum says she won't let me near him til I sort myself out. (laughs sarcastically) She's got a long fuckin wait by the looks of things….

Man 1: My last kid was born a year before I went away. Like a complete dick, I said I wanted nothing to do with her cos I didn't believe she was mine. (to audience) That's between you and me, I'm gonna keep denying her so I don't have to pay no maintenance. I try not to think about them in here cos when I do, it's always bad shit. I imagine how great it would be if my kids and their mam died in a car crash or something cos then I'd get out to attend their funeral…fuck yeh… and I'd get sympathy packages from people.

Man 2: You have all these selfish, asshole thoughts that you can only have when everything good that was ever in your life is slipping away from you.

Man 1: She can walk now, I bet she can talk too, bet she don't ask where her dad is. Wonder what she's been told about me. Wonder if they've told her anything or invented some story about me being in the army and getting killed at war in Afghanistan or some shit like that, or that I got sick and died but I was like this wicked fucking dad before I took my dirt nap. I'm not even sure where they are now, me mam knows but she won't tell me. Kid's probably going to grow up without me. But should she know who I am and why I'm not there? Would it be better to pretend I didn't exist or was dead? Cos I can't help but feel growing up knowing your Dad's an ex-con somehow defines you.

Man 2: The stigma never leaves you. Being homeless defines you. Like that amazing lack of regard or even acknowledgement you get from passers-by. You know I'm here. You know I'm homeless. And you know I'm a person! (pause) In the end it's a matter of well if I get through the day then great, if I don't doesn't matter, no big deal. (pause) It's not like anyone's going to miss whether I'm here or not.

Scene 3: *anger and bargaining*

Man 1: Over the years, specially in prison, if there's one thing I've learned, it's this…

Man 2: Trust no-one.

Man 1: Not even your own fuckin mother!

Man 2: I kept asking - why me?

Man 1: I'd promise when I get out I'll keep on the straight and narrow. I'll be a model fuckin citizen. I aint never ending up back inside.

Man 2: I keep thinking if I can just get a roof over my head…then I'd get a job…I'd quit the drugs. (pause) Then I think if I could just get a job…then I'd get a roof over my head…then I'd quit the drugs.

Man 1: They say that inside you just learn more about crime from the other inmates so you come out worse. What a pile of shit! Are you really going to take advice about crime from someone who got caught?

Man 2: I hear so many bullshit stories your ears would bleed. Everyone has their story. Not that anyone wants to ever fuckin listen anyway. (to audience) You want to hear my story? (pause) See how they all just look away, like if they don't see me I don't exist! So this extreme homeless article is starting to fuck me off now. There was this one story about the homeless billionaire. So this rich prick didn't own a house BUT he lives in hotel suites in top hotels all over the world. That's not fuckin homeless! Apparently, he lost interest in acquiring things cos they didn't satisfy him. So he started paring down his material life, selling off his condo in New York, his mansion in Florida, his cars... Seriously! Yeh I feel right fuckin sorry for him.

Man 1: The fuckers moved me to a prison 200 miles away. Where are my human rights?

Man 2: On the streets you have no fuckin rights at all. Like you're less than human and don't deserve them. Nobody gives a shit!

Man 1: Where are my human rights when my kids and my mum and dad can't come and visit cos it's so bloody far and costs an arm and a leg to get here – they come once a month if I'm fuckin lucky. My missus has the painters in more fuckin regular than visits from my family.

Man 2: You head for a city far from family – don't want to be recognized, don't want them finding you. Though most wouldn't even try, they don't give a shit. Half the people I meet left home cos of the crap that was going on there, the shit they were being put through. Even sleeping rough's better than living with some of that shit. Homelessness is getting a stigma. Everybody thinks that they can't get there. You just don't know. Some people are just one or two paycheques away. Once you're homeless, it becomes nearly impossible to live a normal life. Just getting enough sleep is a struggle. Getting into a shelter's bloody hard cos there's a shortage of beds ... doesn't really offer much relief anyways. Fuckin body lice, nits, snoring, different attitudes, lying down with lights out when you're not even fuckin sleepy ... and then you're there with people with all different kinds of problems, some mental - not that everyone doesn't have their idiosyncrasies, myself included. (laughs ironically) Then in the streets you get blamed and stigmatised for your own fuckin situation – like you went looking for it. Like you made that choice so you deserve whatever fuckin shit you end up with.

Man 1: They say we got it good in here, that the prisons are soft and we've all got our Xboxes, flat screen TVs and all that shit. What the fuck! Winds me up that does. All you're allowed to come in with is the clothes on your back, everything else you've got to get from the prison catalogue and the prices them bastards put on everything you wouldn't fuckin believe. People say we got it so easy cos we don't even have to wear no uniform in this joint – what they don't know is that we have to buy every fuckin item of clothing every fucking toiletry out of the prison catalogue. They're getting rich out of us. And do you know how hard it is to stay such a stylish bastard in here with the crap in those catalogues. Fuck man wouldn't be seen dead in most of that gear!

Man 2: You take whatever you can get, second-hand toiletries...second-hand food! You take whatever clothes you can get to try and keep warm at night.

Man 1: And the boss's fat ass wife is one of them Avon ladies so we got told we could order from Avon too! Like it was some kinda fuckin privilege! I mean it's a fuckin male prison what the fuck are we gonna be buying from Avon? So we end up buying all this shit out of this stupid fuckin Avon magazine and I'm telling you that fat cow must have got enough commission to buy a holiday home in fuckin Majorca! And the worst bit is we'd all be looking in this Avon magazine like a bunch of fuckin gays just to look at the pictures of the women. That's how lonely and shit it gets that your hard-core porn is a fuckin Avon magazine! (pause) You know when I get out if some bitch comes round my door with that Avon magazine I think I'll smash her fuckin face. (pause) well I might cop a feel first (to audience) only kidding.

Man 2: You crave intimacy. It's crazy you spend so much of the day in the streets surrounded by people, even in the hostels they're packed tight yet you feel so utterly miserably alone. You know the best bit about selling the Big Issue isn't the money, it's not even the sense of dignity you get from feeling you're trying to do something about your situation…it's the familiarity of people. You get to know people, their names, their routines, you have your regulars, people who work in the local shops greet you, chat to you, you have moments of conversation. Moments of intimacy with another human being.

Man 1: Everyone inside has their porn stash. Pages of magazines, smuggled porn, that kind of thing. I keep mine under the inner sole of my trainers. You wanna see? (directed at an audience member, waits for response) Fuck off ya perv! You know if you took a survey of what inmates keep for porn you'd be shocked - mostly it's women's faces. The single most sought after item in the common room is the fuckin TV guide cos you get full-page ads for films and beautiful women. Fucking with the TV guide is a hangable offence in here.

Man 2: A conversation that's not a forced one about how you're gonna try and turn things around, that's not about your everyday shit of trying to exist.

Man 1: I guess in the real-world, life's mundane and boring, you need those stereotype porno

	fantasies, dark sexual shit to keep you going. But inside, there's dark shit everywhere.
Man 2:	Violence, death, fear. You don't want it in your head. You try and escape in your head to good decent places, I guess.
Man 1:	You go from having elaborate sexual fantasies, to having sweet, candle lit intimacy fantasies. I fuckin knows it sounds gay mate. Inside, I'd have given anything to know someone loved me - and when I say love, I don't mean like, I'd want to marry them, or that kind of shit. That's a heap… Just that they'd like consent to being intimate with me.
Man 2:	Sometimes you just ride the bus all day, specially if it's raining and shit. Some of the bus drivers are okay but some are fuckin bastards. There's this particular driver who gets off on insulting homeless and manages to make their ride a fuckin nightmare. It's the way he drives, jerking the bus cos he thinks people are sleeping. So he starts jerking and driving faster. Knows where all the bumps and the dips and the curves are and when he gets to those big bumps, he just flies over them. And you can see the sadistic bastard grinning in his mirror.
Man 1:	And another thing there's no fuckin gym equipment in prison. Forget that image. Forget it I'm telling you. Fuckin TV's got a lot to answer for. Gym equipment is a weapon… weapons are forbidden. Our

block's got one treadmill that occasionally works. Add that to high fat food all day, every day, and real quick you're gonna turn into a fat bastard. Not me mind cos I knows how to look after myself (struts about). I mean the ladies gonna be queuing up for a piece of this when I get out and I gotta please my fans. You know you spend most of your day trying to think up some way to do some physical activity. Me and my cellmate deadlift each other for a few hours every day. Gayest thing you've ever seen (pause) but it fills in the time.

Man 2: Your health goes to hell on the streets. Lack of nutrition, drugs, the cold. (pause) Mental health. (pause) Well that's a whole other story. Chicken or egg really. If every day you're looking for food, you're looking for a safe place to live, sooner or later you're going to struggle with your mental health. Even in shelters supposedly safer places … sometimes you get drawn into conflicts even if you don't mean to cos of your behaviour, you're forced to leave the facility. There are just no resources.

Man 1: Fridays, if you can keep track of days, are the absolute worst. It's like our brains are programmed to feel pumped up on a Friday for the start of a weekend…

Man 2: …then you realise that all you have to look forward too was another two days of the same shit.

Man 1: You'd start a fight with anyone, over anything on a Friday.

Man 2: Every day of the week is exactly the same. One day blends into another. You force yourself to get through a day just to reach the end of it.

Man 1: I've seen 6 deaths inside…so far. Two of them were at the hands of screws. Course they'll deny it. Mainly beatings it was, I didn't even know they'd died until later.

Man 2: I've seen a few deaths – drugs, hypothermia - but so many people move on you know, some don't stay in one place too long so you don't know whether they've died or just moved somewhere else or maybe they're one of the few lucky bastards who got off the streets.

Man 1: You know it aint right to call a prison shanking a 'stabbing' cos that's not how you die. Let me educate you here. Inside, we call it 'digging a hole' or 'digging a well' like 'he got a well dug in him' or 'pulled out a hole'. That's cos them makeshift weapons are not easy to kill with. You basically make a hole as fast as you can, by stabbing as fast as you can, and then you try and get a grip inside it and just start pulling.

Man 2: I once saw this guy who died after he'd got the shit beaten out of him. He was in his sleeping bag, all cut and bruised some guys had turned on him when they fell out of a club drunk on a Saturday night and beat him up 'for a laugh'. Turned out he was bleeding internally but nobody knew til next morning when he wasn't moving. Turned him over. He'd been dead a while and he'd turned blue it was so fuckin freezing.

Man 1: I saw it right up close one time. Once these two guys were loitering around near my cell one day, waiting for this fresh kid to wander past. Prison gossip said he'd been worked over on his first night by someone who wanted him for a wife, but the kid fought back and nearly bit some fucker's nuts off. So his friends wait with a t-shirt, and a filed down toothbrush. They've cracked down on plastic toothbrushes, but there used to be enough of them that a lot of guys have them stashed away. You can file down the ends on the concrete to a point. One guy wrapped a t-shirt round the kid's neck and lifted him off the ground from behind, and the other starts stabbing his gut. After a few stabs, he starts trying to get his fingers inside and he just pulls all this meat out. I thought he was going to pull out his intestines like you'd see in a horror film, but instead, he just pulls out fist after fist of this yellow jelly shit, and then big hunks of meat like raw mince.

Man 2: Just looked at him and thought, lucky bastard at least it's over for you.

Man 1: Screw's arrived and tasered everyone. Even the kid. He was on his side, right in front of my cell, and every jolt from the taser made the big hole in his stomach smoke. You don't see something like that and not have it fuck you up worse than you already were for being in the fuckin joint.

Man 2: It's a constant struggle for dignity.

Man 1: So yeah. People are not friendly inside.

Man 2: A constant struggle against a system that doesn't work.

Man 1: An endless shit fight of politics and fuckery.

Scene 4: *depression, reflection, loneliness…*

Man 1: Literacy levels in prison are fucking awful. A lot of inmates end up teaching themselves how to read because there aint much else to do apart from get a library book and that's not much fuckin use if you can't read and their writing is fucking horrendous.

Man 2: Filling out forms is overwhelming. You don't know where to begin and you need to fill out forms for everything. They think the problem is you can't read or write. Of course I can fuckin read and write! I just don't know where to begin. I start filling in this form and then realise I've been staring at it for an hour and haven't got past the first question. Or one question throws you, you know, even a simple fuckin question like what your address is. Simple fuckin questions for anyone else but….

Man 1: My cellmate's 'functionally illiterate', fuckin retard in other words, got nothing else to do so I help him write letters for his appeals and to his daughter. Don't go thinking it's some bonding crap. It aint no Dead Poet's Society moment or nothing - I aint teaching him how to write and we don't hold hands and feel the love and all that shit.

Man 2: It's all just ways to pass the fuckin time, trying to forget all the fuckin labels and judgement.

Man 1: You're a con, an ex-offender…

Man 2: A smackhead, homeless. Every label carries a load of shit with it. People look at you and don't ask themselves how you ended up homeless,

Man 1: how you ended up inside

Man 2: No! They just look at you and judge you for being in that situation.

Man 1: …judge you for who they think that makes you.

Man 2: You go through these periods of just feeling shit, sorry for yourself, crap like and it's normal, so don't be "talked out of it" by well-meaning outsiders. It's not fuckin helpful.

Man 1: This group came in to give us sessions on how to rebuild our lives on the outside. They just randomly picked 15 of us at a time to go and sit there for two fuckin hours listening to their crap. Only three of us were ever getting out, the rest were all lifers. Prison's full of sessions from fuckers like that and you get points for attending so you sign up ...

Man 2: ... you sure as fuck earn your points listening to that crap. I mean people telling me where I went wrong and how to make sure it never happens again, how to pick myself up and start again!

Man 1: What the fuck do they know about me or why I'm inside?

Man 2: You finally realize the true magnitude of everything you've lost and it depresses the fuck out of you. You focus on memories of the past, like searching for a time when it was better.

Man 1: Convincing yourself it was better even when it wasn't.

Man 2: You just feel empty.

Man 1: It's the uncertainty that gets to you. The loneliness.

Man 2: The unbearable loneliness.

Man 1: You know on TV you see all these groups of guys in prison hanging out. Bullshit! No one hangs with any more than three people cos if you're seen with a big group, you'll be targeted by the screws. Mostly, people see

	out their time alone. Pacing the yard, or even just ignoring their cellmates completely.
Man 2:	That gets to you more than anything. The constant suspicion and knowing you're alone no matter how many people are around you.
Man 1:	No one ever talks about it cos prison makes you a hard ass. Or at least that's what you tell yourself to believe.
Man 2:	The first ones to go are your friends.
Man 1:	They tell you they'll write and send you stuff - take every friend you've ever had, now pick one. There will be one that actually does it. But they'll stop after a few months.
Man 2:	They let you sofa surf. They're sympathetic…for a while. Then you start getting the looks, like why can't you sort yourself out, when are you gonna get somewhere to stay and leave them the fuck alone.
Man 1:	Then your missus – she says she'll wait, but you know she won't. I can't stand spending every night wondering if she's getting cranked by some other bastard so I'd rather just end it.
Man 2:	One less thing to worry about. My kid will never know who the fuck I am. His mam took him away the second she could. Never called. Don't even know where to begin looking for them.

Man 1: Prison makes you realise just how much we rely on digital photographs, know what I mean. I realised I didn't have any hard copies before I went away, everything was on my computer or my phone. My photo of my kids is a folded-up piece of paper printed out before I left.

Man 2: Photos are just ways of reminding you of everything you've lost.

Man 1: My Mum and Dad were the worst. They promised me when I went inside that they'd stick by me. I was so fucked up half the time I forgot when visiting day even was. I realised and tried to tell the boss that I didn't want to see them, that I was too messed up. So the cunts dragged me by the hair through the block to the visiting room and propped me up on a chair in front of them and just laughed. My parents never came back.

Man 2: It's not so much that they rejected me. They didn't. I just don't know how to face them or what I'd say. I feel it's just too late now. I guess I rejected them. (laughs)

Man 1: As for friends in the joint… I never had one.

Man 2: You can't trust anyone. You don't make real friendships on the street. And in the hostels, you know what everyone wants more than anything else? A pair of decent fuckin shoes! So the minute you take your shoes off you know you might never see them again. That some bastard who seemed like your

	best friend five minutes ago will thief those fuckers soon as look at you.
Man 1:	I seen this TV shit about what it's like inside. Bull! What they don't tell you is how fuckin depressing it is, how the endless time eats away at you cos all you got time to do in prison is think... about your kids, your missus, what you done. Think about what a fuckin loser you are.
Man 2:	You know on the telly you see all these miserable homeless bastards hanging around a fire like it's some kind of fuckin scout outing? Well I can tell you on the streets it's about you, looking after you, looking after anything you own cos it'll get thieved in a second. That and watching out you don't get raped when you eventually manage to fall asleep.
Man 1:	And then you close your eyes and pray sleep will come just so you can stop fuckin thinking. Then there's that moment when you first wake up that you don't remember where you are and you feel good...for a fraction of a second you feel good. Then reality hits.

Scene 5: *the upward turn?*

Man 1:	After two years, I feel like I got the whole prison kick down. I feel like I belongs. New guys look up to me, like someone who's seen shit and made it through. I start getting this kind of Zen calm about incarceration.

	I'm the urban Bear Grylls! The last two months before I left was the happiest of my entire miserable fuckin life. I started making lists. Lists of what I was going to do. Know what I mean? Like if it was you what would you wanna do as soon as you got out? (directs the question to Man2 and to random audience members, pushing them to answer)
Man 2:	Every day I started making lists of what I wanted. Lists of things I was going to eat. Like… (give some examples, engage with Man1 and audience throughout the section)
Man 1:	Got to be Nandos for me. (describes exactly what he would eat in detail). You know a while back I got my wallet stolen and you know what pissed me off most, my Nandos loyalty card was in it and the bastard took it! I mean I can replace my bank cards but my Nandos card! They gave me a new one but had to start from zero on it. I was seriously fuckin vexed. Told them they needed to give me my rewards and this kid on the phone says how does he know I'm telling the truth. I fuckin lost it then and the bastard said he was banning me from all Nandos for a year! How the fuck are you gonna do that you little shit? Gonna put a wanted picture in every fuckin Nandos in the whole country? Told him he better grow some eyes on the back of his head cos I was gonna find him and…
Man 2:	Lists of places I was going to go. You know if I could go anywhere, if you had that

freedom. I've got lists everywhere, I keep thinking if I write it down it's more real and there's a chance. (pause) You've got to believe it's possible.

Man 1: You've got to start somewhere. Thing is when you're inside, you feel you've lost everything, you stop dreaming…

Man 2: You stop believing anything good could ever happen to you…

Man 1: You've got to let yourself dream again.

Man 2: Start with the small stuff.

Man 1: I started planning everything for when I'd finally get out, what I was going to do, what I'd eat, drink, where I'd go, what I'd spend every penny I got on, who I'd see…

Man 2: I wanted to reconstruct my life.

Man 1: I almost felt like I'd had a near death experience and now I had to live a better life. (pause) Then I fuckin left. (pause) What can I say? Two years is a long time.

Man 2: The world literally changes without you.

Man 1: I got off the bus and went to my favourite pub. It was empty. I went to a cafe my friends used to touch dicks at. None of them were there. I just stood around like a spare fuckin bollocks.

Man 2: It was so fuckin depressing realizing everything and everyone had moved on without me.

Man 1: Went to some hostel and sat on the edge of the bed, watching TV and ordering Pizza. I must have ordered like five pizzas from five different places, stayed up till dawn.

Man 2: So this extreme fuckin homelessness piece of shit article. There's another story about this guy in the States who lived in this woman's attic for 5 months undetected. When she'd go to work, he'd come down and make himself something to eat, shower and shit. He had set it all up with a bed and everything and had peep holes so he knew when he could come downstairs!!! I mean give me a fuckin break! That isn't extreme homelessness, it's not homelessness of any kind, do you know what that is?

Man 1: It's fuckin stalking that's what it is! Different labels, different perspectives. (pause) And the system grinds you down, labels you

Man 2: and you walk around with that label like it's a fuckin target on your back.

Man 1: You got to keep fighting the system

Man 2: You've got to vote for the change you want…

Man 1: What the fuck you on about mate? Vote! If voting made a difference they wouldn't let us do it! Think about it!

Man 2: So what's your big plan then?

Man 1: Right now? Right now man my big plan is to get a good night's fuckin sleep. You know one of the things about prison is that sleep's like a chore you do each day.

Man 2: You're never really tired, so you never really want to sleep, it just breaks up the time.

Man 1: I feel like I don't ever want to sleep again.

Man 2: I just wandered around for a day. Felt like everyone was staring at me.

Man 1: I just felt lost.

Man 2: Completely lost.

Man 1: You know it's not the being inside that screws you up mentally, it's adjusting when you get out.

Man 2: It's trying to change, the first steps, trying not to slip back … and when you do, not seeing it as the end. (pause) Sometimes it takes a lot of beginnings.

Man 1: Adjusting to space – so much space. You're so used to not having it so it feels scary. Queues that was what did it for me. I spent two years, 3 months and 17 days queuing for every fucking thing I did. Perfect single file fuckin queues. Then I gets out and no bastard in this country knows how to fuckin queue. Straight lines! Single file! Is that so fuckin hard? Does my head in!

Man 2: When I first started selling The Big Issue, I was ashamed, didn't want anyone who knew me to see me doing it. Eventually I thought, well it's honest. I'm trying to sell something, trying to do something about my situation, I'm not just standing out there asking for money. (pause) But there's always the stigma of homelessness. A lot of people are nice to me, but then you have the dickheads that look at you like you're fuckin contagious. You don't have to give me money. Some people don't have it neither, I get that. But, you know, the acknowledgement, the smile, the speaking, being courteous …that doesn't hurt anyone. Whether you buy a copy or not, I'm always going to tell you, 'Have a nice day.' they're telling me, 'No, not today,' cos they've already decided that I'm about to ask for something so they don't listen to what I'm actually saying.

Man 1: So I hops on the bus back to the hostel and waited up all night for morning. Because when I close my eyes I'm terrified I'm going to wake up back in my cell, listening to wheezy ass coughs, sniffling and crying, grunting, someone wanking off and the ever-present deviated septum snoring of my cellmate.

Man 2: It's a stupid fear, but once it's dark, I get this creeping terror …

Man 1: That maybe I'm still there, that this is all a fevered dream and when I wake up, I'll still be inside.

Scene 6: *reconstruction & working through*

Man 2: Anyway you're probably thinking this has all been pretty grim shit.

Man 1: So I'm thinking let's make a list of the best things about freedom. Not sappy bullshit… just the real simple stuff you take for granted til you aint got it no more.

Man 2: …things you probably take for granted cos you've never had them taken away. What would it be for you? Things like laughter.

Man 1: No one really laughs on the inside. You might occasionally fake a laugh when someone does something stupid or gets what they deserve. But inside nothing's really funny when you're locked in a concrete bunker with seemingly no hope of getting out. When I went inside, my favourite things were horror movies and violent video games. Now I can't stand the thought of them.

Man 2: I've seen too much real violence for one lifetime. I liked to think that I used to be funny, but now, I realise I'm not. I look in the mirror and there is this kind of grimness there. Don't take laughter for granted. It can be taken away so easily.

Man 1: Here's another one for you - politeness. We all think we're such fucking bad asses that we don't need to use manners. I used to be the biggest offender. But inside, it just starts to grate on you after a while - that you're forced to be polite to the boss, but your daily interactions with convicts are typified by cursing, shoving, and basically barbaric behaviour.

Man 2: Basic human decency becomes the thing you miss the most. Greeting people and being acknowledged by them, saying 'please' and 'thank you' and 'you're welcome' just simple shit like that reminds you you're human, that you're a part of society.

Man 1: When I first got out, I kept saying please and thank you all the time. People thought I was hitting on them (pause) or that I was a fuckin retard. The thing I've enjoyed most since I've left are just simple normal interactions with people. Paying for the bus – well except for finding out how fuckin expensive it had got in two years. Talking to the person you're sitting next to.

Man 2: Buying a sandwich. Excusing yourself when you pass someone in the street. Helping people.

Man 1: I helped a woman get a pushchair off the bus this morning, and she probably walked away

	thinking 'what a nice young man', she'd no idea I've just spent two years locked inside a cesspool of fuckin human indignity. That made me feel good about myself.
Man 2:	Being nice makes you feel good about yourself
Man 1:	See on the inside - you never feel good about yourself.
Man 2:	Clothes. I will never wear the same clothes two days in a row for as long as I live. I'm a stylish mother fucker I am.
Man 1:	Inside, I had two pairs of elastic tracky bottoms, two t-shirts, a jumper and a jacket with the buttons taken off. Four pairs of boxers. Two pairs of laceless trainers - might try and kill someone else or myself if they let me keep them apparently - and a pair of flip-flops.
Man 2:	In winter, I'd wear every piece of clothing I had all at the same time.
Man 1:	When I left, I gave my prison clothes to another inmate for some toothpaste. On the outside I realised how all my old clothes were so dark and I desperately wanted colour in my life. Like a Hawaiian shirt or some shit like that, didn't give a damn if I'd look fuckin gay.
Man 2:	Clothes make you feel better about your place in the universe. Just wearing jeans that fit is a major event.

Man 1: Being allowed to own a belt. Having nice shoes.

Man 2: Never take that shit for granted. It's not like I was ever a fucking fashion plate or anything, but now I have this new-found appreciation for looking nice.

Man 1: They taught me how to sew inside. I've been wondering if I couldn't maybe become a tailor or something. The world's first straight, ex-con fashion designer.

Man 2: The last thing you should never take for granted is your mental health.

Man 1: Every day I woke up sober, at some points, they were rare, I'd stare at the ceiling and talk to myself. Sometimes out loud.

Man 2: I'd take stock of my own level of madness. How justified was my paranoia today? What did I dream of last night? What kind of bad things will float through my head if I don't control it? I'd literally have to take stock of my own psychological well-being. No one should have to do that.

Man 1: Questioning your sanity is like picking at a scab - once you start it bleeding you can't help but keep picking. I went more than a little crazy inside.

Man 2: The insane amount of smack I ingested might have had something to do with it.

Man 1: For me, the punishment of prison was less about separation, and more about the forced introspection.

Man 2: It's kind of like a forced autism, only without being any kind of savant.

Man 1: That's what prison is. Outside, you're free to keep your head in check. You're free to indulge your mind and keep it healthy. And I guess if you keep your mind healthy, you'll be less inclined to find yourself inside in the first place.

Scene 7: *acceptance and hope*

Man 2: Accept and deal with the reality of your situation. (pause) Acceptance doesn't mean instant happiness.

Man 1: … you don't say.

Man 2: Face it, you know you can never return to the carefree, untroubled YOU that existed before this tragedy.

Man 1: I'm not sure I was ever a carefree, untroubled fucker.

Man 2: You like…well… you find a way forward. You've got to.

Man 1: You make a decision that you're gonna trust. Like a conscious decision, you just gotta take that step or you get paranoid and think everyone's out to get you and everyone's looking at you.

Man 2: It's a choice. And you start to realise that ultimately everything's been a choice – the good and the bad.

Man 1: One of the few things about prison I ever seen in a film that I kinda vibes with - can't remember which film it was - was this line about there being 'inmates' and 'convicts'. How an 'inmate' is a prisoner, they're scared and they want to get out and never go back. A 'convict' knows, deep down, they're a criminal, that through their actions they've placed themselves outside the 'man's' law, and that status defines them. Prison does a wicked job of scaring the shit out of the inmate. But convicts... Don't get me wrong, I never want to go back. (pause) But as I reflect on it, I've almost found a special pride in having made it through.

Man 2: I was at a bus stop this morning and I started chatting with someone about how the bus was late, what she was listening to on her iPod ... just random shit. And as we got on the bus I suddenly realised ... that was me ...that was me from before talking ... I'm still that same person.

Man 1: I was really proud for having wrapped that part of me up when I was on the inside that I kept it safe. (pause) It doesn't make me ever want to go back.

Man 2: If you make it off the streets you've got an incentive...an incentive to never ever end up back there again.

Man 1: For a lot of cons, I think what brings them back is the adrenalin rush more than anything. Committing a serious crime is a big ass rush, but life inside keeps you riding this constant edge - some people would get off on the paranoia, the violence, the constant tension. You'd probably find a lot of parallels between the kinds of guys who keep signing up for tours through war zones and the kinds of guys who keeping winding up back inside.

Man 2: Some people are just on an endless cycle. I know I don't want that to be me. I'm just glad that the merry-go-round of bullshit they have me on keeps me busy enough to not want to use. Ironically though, going to those fuckin NA meetings makes me want to use more. I mean listening to these people whine on endlessly about how their habits have ruined their lives and how God is helping them recover...

Man 1: Drink and drugs didn't ruin my life. In fact, had I had an endless supply, I would never have committed the crime I went inside for.

Man 2: You don't ruin your life on drugs or alcohol. You ruin your life when you're not on them. You might ruin your life when you're trying to score for more - but that's your own, sober responsibility. Blaming anything on drugs or drink is stupid. An abdication of personal responsibility. 'I ruined my baby's life on drugs' they say. I feel like jumping up and saying: Fuck you, no one ever got pregnant while high, no one can fuck on the nod, you got pregnant sober, probably whoring for more crack, and it should have been enough for you to stop using but you didn't.

Man 1: As for God, who seems intent on being name checked every thirty fuckin seconds at every meeting, I really don't think He cares about anyone's drug use.

Man 2: If I was God, I'd have bigger concerns than a few junkies and an ex-piss-head ex-con.

Man 1: My parole officer thinks he's fuckin God. He says I'm arrogant. And I'm thinking what a prick. You know my parole office is next door to Wetherspoons. I mean for fucks sake, of all the fuckin places they could put my parole office and they choose a fuckin Wetherspoons! I fucked up my own life. With my own choices. I acknowledged that in a courtroom, I signed confessions for that. I spent two years in hell making up for that. And now some guy in a bad suit and a sweat-stained shirt in an office can send me back for another two years for that if he decides to make my life difficult. I walked away from it with my sanity just about intact and strangely enough no great desire to keep drinking and I think that entitles me to a degree of arrogance when subjected to the literal dregs of humanity.

Man 2: It's about learning to trust again. Learning to turn off that noise in your head ... or learn to make friends with it. Know what I mean.

Man 1: When you're inside, you know that no one is coming to help you. (pause) When you get out you don't know how to ask for help anymore.

Man 2: And the Red Cross isn't going to knock on your door one day and bring you a fuckin gift basket. God himself isn't going to reach down and pluck you out of your punishment cos you're pious,

Man 1: or cos you accepted Jesus Christ as your personal lord, saviour and catchall excuse for being a stupid fucker.

Man 2: But so many fucking losers believe that shit.

Man 1: They think they're entitled to some second chance because some guy tells them 'how much progress' they're making each day and they show off their fucking sobriety coins.

Man 2: I don't respect them, so I won't listen to them. When it's my time to share in the stupid fuckin meetings, I recite platitudes and 'drug free' rhetoric until it's time to stop. That's what they want to hear and I'm fuckin great at it. I should've been an actor. Then I mainline free coffee, sign my name and get the fuck out of there.

Man 1: I was in town watching this armoured van pull up. I watched the guards carry these huge platters of cash in and start re-filling the cash points. I started thinking how easy it would be… How I'd park between their van and the front doors and have them covered before they realised what was happening - how I'd probably only need one other person with me to cover the guy they probably had in the back with a shotgun - how you could get one, maybe two grand out of them, on the Thursday or Friday before a holiday weekend. That's enough to disappear with.

Man 2: I saw this junkie lying in a doorway. I was staring at him without realising, thinking how that's me. That's me lying there. He looks up and asks me for some money for a cuppa and I laugh. The irony of it just got to me. And he loses it and shouts, 'fuck off you tight bastard!'. And I thought of all the shit I could have said to him but I knew he wouldn't listen. I wouldn't have.

Man 1: I thought about how I could do it better than last time, how I wouldn't make the same stupid mistakes. Then the cops drove by and I shat myself. Hadn't done a thing and I shits myself. I felt this panic wash over me, like they might know what I was thinking. Like they were in my fucking mind. (laughs)

Man 2: Sometimes I sit up all night, waiting for morning to come.

Man 1: When I close my eyes, I'm terrified I'm going to wake up back in my cell, listening to those fuckin wheezy ass coughs, crying, grunting, someone wanking off and the ongoing deviated septum snoring of my cellmate.

Man 2:   It's a stupid fear, but once it's dark, I get this creeping terror that maybe I'm still there

Man 1:   that this is all a fevered dream and when I wake up I'll still be inside.

Man 2:   And that makes me angry, angry as hell!

Man 1:   And that gives me hope cos for the first time in fuckin forever I'm feeling something.

The End

Workshop Ideas

Below are discussion points and exercises that can help not only lead us to a better understanding of the play, but also of Applied Theatre and what it involves. In all Applied Theatre and Theatre of the Oppressed exercises, discussion is key. Always allow ample time for discussion after each exercise and explore what has happened.

Discussion questions

1. Discuss the stage elements of the play and what makes it Applied Theatre e.g. set, lights, props etc.
2. The concept of applied plays is not to take sides but simply to tell the story. How do our feelings about the two men change throughout and why?
3. Each scene carries the title of one of the seven stages of bereavement. Why do you think the characters' experiences are being described under these headings? What do you think the playwright's intent was in doing this?
4. The play uses strong language and the characters make many politically incorrect statements. How does this serve the play? Why do you think this was necessary?
5. 'The play ends with the final stage of bereavement and gives us a sense of hope for the future as a result.' Discuss.
6. What is the purpose of this play?
7. The set is designed to make an audience feel entrapped. How do you think this is achieved in this play where there is no set whatsoever?
8. Discuss why you think both of these men wanted their stories to be told.
9. What feelings is the writer trying to evoke in the audience in scenes that are violently graphic? Why?

10. 'If you are not actively doing something about these issues, then you are part of the problem.' Discuss.
11. Moments of humour are key to many applied scripts in order to give the audience a moment of release. Look at the humorous moments in the play and what preceded them. Why was it so important to include humour at those precise moments?
12. When the audience laughs in applied theatre, they become complicit. What do you think is meant by this?
13. We are never told why **Man 1** was incarcerated or why **Man 2** became homeless. Is it relevant to know this information? Would it influence our feelings towards them in any way?
14. In scene 1 each character details their current possessions. What do their possessions tell us about them?
15. Scene 5 is entitled 'the upward turn' and is followed by a question mark. Why do you think this is?
16. 'The humour in this play is satirical and indirectly making a commentary on society and on the audience.' Discuss.
17. Discuss the distortion of time for each of the characters.
18. The play explores labelling – the idea that society gives us labels and we are invisible beyond that label and the stigma it brings. Discuss.
19. The characters often say things to shock the listener. What do you think is the playwright's intention in doing this?
20. It is normal for an Applied Theatre performance to have a discussion time with the audience after the play. Why do you think this is necessary?
21. It has been said that Applied Theatre plays with our emotion and our certainties. Discuss.

Applied Theatre Exercises

When doing these exercises it is important to remember that the different stages will often be carried out on different days and do not need to be done in succession. The exercises can be adapted and used for any of the plays.

Please note that in Applied Theatre time should *always* be allocated to discuss and process the exercises after they have been completed.

A Sense of Belonging

Two actors assume the roles of the characters. They sit apart in a space on the stage to represent their setting (prison and the street). With their eyes closed, they take it in turn to work through each of their five senses to describe their setting (what they can see, hear, smell, taste and touch).

A Change of Scenery (Part 1)

When doing these exercises it is important to remember that the different stages will often be carried out on different days and do not need to be done in succession.

Stage 1: Mark out an area on stage to represent a prison cell and another to represent the street. Have actors, in character, sit in their respective areas. Each will then:

- Pace the space repeatedly to get a feel for its limiting size, exploring the limitations of movement and comfort.
- One is confined to a set space with the size of the cell; the other is in an open

street. Yet both are confined and imprisoned in certain ways. Have each character explore their own concept of being restricted/imprisoned.
- Explore the thoughts that the confines of their space brings to them.
- Each character shares thoughts on how the space affects them emotionally and mentally. How might this change in the short and long term?

As a group discuss what you learned about the space; how it made you feel. How do you think both character's situations would affect you?

Stage 2: The characters swap places. They are now in one another's situation. Now repeat all of stage 1. Discuss how perceptions may change when we are in a situation as opposed to hearing about it.

Stage 3: This time both characters stay in the same place (first base both in the prison, then repeat the stage with them based in the street). Explore the different elements of stage 1 together, discussing and questioning one another in the process. Discuss how sharing an experience can change our perception of it and how it can change our focus. Does it make us more or less empathetic? Are we limited by our own ego focusing on ourselves before others? What does this tell you about the society the two men are surrounded by?

A Change of Scenery (Part 2)

When doing these exercises it is important to remember that the different stages will often be carried out on different days and do not need to be done in succession.

Stage 1: Make a list of **likely places** the two characters might be seen in (for example, a court room, a shop, a park, a support group, a counselling session and so on).

Stage 2: One actor in character creates an image of one such scene, inserting himself at the end. On a signal from the facilitator the scene comes alive for 1-2 minutes, then the facilitator claps for it to freeze. While frozen contemplate what has happened so far, how did the character feel in this situation (threatened, angry, out-of-place etc.). On a signal from the facilitator the scene resumes once more. Continue this process for a period of time. Repeat for different settings for each of the actors. Discuss after each scene.

Stage 3: Repeat stage 2 but now both characters discuss and make the image, inserting themselves when it is complete. We now have both characters in one scene. Watch how the dynamics change – do they interact with, or avoid one another? Discuss after each scene.

A Change of Scenery (Part 3)

When doing these exercises it is important to remember that the different stages will often be carried out on different days and do not need to be done in succession.

Stage 1: Make a list of **unlikely places** the two characters might be seen in (for example, an expensive restaurant, a museum, a theatre, an aeroplane journey and so on).

Stage 2: One actor (in character) creates an image of one such scene, inserting himself at the end. On a signal from the facilitator the scene comes alive for 1-2 minutes, then the facilitator claps for it to freeze. While frozen contemplate what has happened so far, how does the character feel in this situation (threatened, angry etc.). On a signal from the facilitator the scene resumes once more. Continue this process for a period of time. Repeat for different setting for each of the actors. Discuss after each scene.

Stage 3: Repeat stage 2 but now both characters discuss and make the image, inserting themselves when it is complete. We now have both characters in one scene. Watch how the dynamics change – do they interact with, or avoid one another? Discuss after each scene.

Behind the Label

Stage 1: One actor, in character, stands in front of six others. He brings one in front and moulds him to represent the main label that he has been given by society. For example, he might choose prisoner, homeless, addict, or alcoholic.

The other 5 actors are now behind the 'label'. The character ponders who he is behind that label and moulds the five actors into 5 things he is that nobody sees because of his label. For example, a father, a worker, honest, talented, loyal and so on.

Stage 2: Once all have been moulded the sculptor gives each one a word to describe them. He then approaches each in turn and speaks to them about who they are, including the label that he has been stigmatised by at the front. The statues listen but remain frozen.

Stage 3: The sculptor returns to speak to the images and this time they can also speak (although they must remain frozen). They can ask questions, demand more information, empathise, challenge…

When the sculptor no longer wishes to engage with one he moves to another. Only the actor he is speaking to can engage in conversation with him. The others must remain silent.

Stage 4: Repeat stage 3 only this time once the sculptor has engaged with the statues their voices remain activated. Even when the sculptor moves away they can continue to speak and try to get him to return to them.

The noise level will increase making it difficult to sustain any conversation. The sculptor may feel torn and confused. The exercise is intended to bring out all of these feelings which are true representations of what he must feel. The statues are true to who they are but this will often mean that the statue representing the 'label' is the loudest and drowns out the others. Afterwards discuss how this happens in real life. That is, how the label becomes the main thing or only thing people see.

Stage 5: The statues remain in their positions and the sculptor steps away. All the statues begin a discussion among themselves. They remain frozen but they can all communicate. By remaining frozen the label can never turn to look at the others. This is symbolic of how all-consuming the label can be and what he represents in that person. For example if the label is addict, when the character is in full addiction he does not see or hear anyone, the addiction drives him and leads him to ignore so many other aspects of himself. The idea being that society stigmatizes us with labels, but we also stigmatize ourselves.

The other statues could be pleading with him, trying to convince him to give them a position in front.

Stage 6: The label is removed and the remaining statues discuss what they need to do to remove the label permanently. What would it take? What would they need to do? How might they convince him to go away?

Stage 7: The label returns and based on what they have discussed in stage 6, the statues try to convince him why he should leave. The statue listens and argues his case to stay as the most prominent and important label. However if he feels the others convince him he can move by exiting the image.

Stage 8: All statues return to their original positions. On a signal from the facilitator the actor (in character) enters and remoulds them if he feels they have changed throughout the events above. After remoulding them, he gives each either the same word they had before, or a new one if he believes it is appropriate. Finally he repositions them one behind the other in a line – the one he believes to be most prominent at the front and the others in decreasing order behind.

My Younger self

Stage 1: Two actors sit facing one another. One is in character, the other is his 5-year-old self. The one in character is given 5 minutes to give his younger self all the advice he can think of. The character knows what lies ahead so must try to advise/teach/guide the other. The child listens but does not speak.

Stage 2: Stage 1 is repeated. The actor in character begins to repeat everything he said in stage 1, however this time he has fifteen minutes to do so. The 5-year-old can now respond. It is essential that the 5-year-old responds like a small child. He must have the child's level of comprehension, vocabulary and attention span. The exercise becomes frustrating for the character and the attempt to simplify things, or avoid others means he will have probably have very little success getting his message across.

Stage 3: Stages 1 and 2 are repeated only now the character is sitting in front of his teenage self. When the teenager is allowed to speak, he may be arrogant, unwilling to listen to someone he views as 'an old person', thinking he knows best. Explore teenage attitudes and how the character tries to get through to his teenage self.

Stage 4: Stages 1 and 2 are repeated only now the character is facing his current self. Look at the intricacies of how they talk to one another and their ability/inability to listen to what the other is saying.

Stage 5: In this closing stage the character is now facing his older self. This time the older self speaks for the 5 minutes and the character remains silent. In the next part the older self repeats but the character can now engage in discussion.

Conclusion

Through Applied Theatre we came to understand was the notion of perception, of how we all see things differently based on our own knowledge, emotions and experience. More importantly our interpretation at any given time, for time and experience could come to change it, is not wrong. There is no right or wrong involved in applied work, simply an understanding that we all see the world and its situations differently. It is about telling the stories of real people and their real situations, giving a voice. That may seem very obvious and on one level it certainly is, however, the implications that accompany it are immense and complex.

If we all understand the world differently, if perception is key to our translation of circumstance, then how do we deal with issues that involve us and our community without essentially recognising that we are all approaching such issues differently? And is not theatre one of the most accessible, open and safest arenas to explore these different perspectives? Is not theatre a place to show that different perspectives exist, and it is not about right or wrong but about exploring this and seeking to gain a better understanding of ourselves and our community? The plays in this book, the discussions and the exercises are intended to explore all of these issues.

Applied Theatre takes us on a journey, one for which there is no final destination. We hope you have enjoyed accompanying us on this journey.

Printed in Great Britain
by Amazon